To Ch...
Bes... ...
Juliet Michaels

An Irish

Passion

JULIET MICHAELS

Copyright © 2015 Frisky Publications

Cover Images © 2015 Szefei – Depositphotos.com

ISBN: 1516852125
ISBN-13: 978-1516852123

CONTENTS

PART ONE

CHAPTER ONE

Jane looked at her twin sister with amazement.

"I can't believe you've done this," she said.

They were in the small Italian restaurant where they occasionally met. Victoria had rung and said she wanted to meet after work as she had something to tell Jane and she wanted to surprise her. Jane had been on edge since she received the call. As twins, they were no longer particularly close, and Jane was uneasily wondering what this was all about. Of course, it had been different when they were young, sharing a bedroom, playing together, dressing alike and occasionally tricking people into wondering which twin was which. However, time had changed all that, their paths had followed different ways, and the old easy intimacy was not always there.

Victoria was in control, dressed in a fitted, expensive navy suit, designer handbag on the seat beside her and mobile phone placed neatly on duty next to her plate in case she was needed. Jane slumped back, her jeans uncomfortably tight around her waist, and her cotton blouse creased. She knew that she shouldn't even have looked at the dessert menu, but she'd been unable to resist that tempting lemon torte. As usual, she felt at a disadvantage when she was with her immaculate, slim sister; their lives and circumstances were so different now. This time her anger was only just below the surface and was in danger of bubbling up.

"You've really gone and arranged a double birthday party without even asking me?" she exclaimed.

"Well, we *are* thirty in two weeks time, and, be honest, you haven't arranged anything yourself, have you?" Victoria replied calmly. She knew that she was right.

Jane hadn't made any plans for her birthday, and she usually got her own way without any problems.

"And you've actually had the cheek to ask people and tell them not to say anything to me?" Jane continued.

"It was meant to be a surprise," Victoria explained, "but then I thought I should tell you just in case, by any chance, you were going out. Mum and Dad will be there, all the grandparents and close relatives, your friends, my friends, work colleagues. Don't worry. Julian and I will be paying for it. You only have to turn up. What could be better?"

Jane sat up straight, reached for her glass of Chablis and swallowed a swift gulp, trying – and not succeeding – in hiding her irritation.

"What could be better," Jane replied, "would be for you to have your own party with all your yuppy friends and leave me to do exactly what I want to do on my own birthday."

"Which would probably be a cheap take-away, followed by quick sex with that waste of time Greg," Victoria snapped. She was not used to being challenged and Jane was pleased to see that she'd actually become a little flushed and ruffled.

"And have you asked him to this event?" Jane said.

She knew that Greg, who she'd been seeing for the last year, was not going to be on any party list drawn up by her twin. And although she secretly agreed that he *was* a bit of a waste of space, she still felt slightly annoyed on his behalf.

Victoria sipped her mineral water, then glanced at her mobile, as if hoping it might ring and rescue her from this awkward moment.

"Be reasonable," she said, speaking as if addressing a board meeting. "We have the same birthday, thirty is a bit of a milestone, so why not celebrate together? It's a meal at a great hotel, a fabulous birthday cake, champagne, music afterwards. You only have to turn up, and if you really want to you can go early, after my announcement."

Ah, here it was! The real reason for the special party. Victoria had something to announce and as usual would have arranged things so that she would be centre stage. What would this announcement be? Julian's promotion to a job abroad? A move to an even bigger house? An important career change for Victoria?

"Well, as I'm not going to be there," Jane said, slumping even further down in her seat, "so you might as well tell me now." Once again she was probably going to be over-shadowed by her brilliant twin.

Victoria took another sip of her water and then placed the glass carefully down on the table.

"Actually, I'm pregnant," she said. "I'm going to tell everyone at the party."

"Pregnant?" Jane was astounded "I didn't know you planned to have a family!"

"Of course we did," Victoria replied, smiling slightly. "When the time was right. And that happens to be now."

Jane took another large gulp of wine whilst she thought over this surprising news. Victoria and Julian always seemed to have the perfect life - interesting, fabulously paid jobs, a large detached house in leafy Wimbledon, travel to exciting locations, a holiday cottage in Cornwall and a host of friends. How would a baby fit in, Jane wondered. All those broken nights, nappies to be changed, sore nipples from breast feeding.

She looked at her perfectly composed twin. She would always love her, and they had a bond which had held them together since their birth, but, sometimes she still felt completely irritated with Victoria. Of course she would be one of those mothers who Tweeted and Facebooked endlessly, each tiny baby problem discussed and analysed at length, and information shared around. She would have every possible piece of baby equipment ever invented and probably an au pair as well!

"So, as usual, this is all about you, not really about sharing a birthday party," Jane said, the words leaping out before she could stop herself and she only realised afterwards just how mean she sounded.

But Victoria didn't seem to be too concerned.

"It's about both," she said. "Look, I realise that we haven't seen much of each other lately, and I know we lead different lives, but I thought about this some time ago, a shared celebration. And when the baby comes, you could become involved, be a special aunt."

Grudgingly Jane held up her glass. "Well, congratulations, and sorry about being so grumpy."

"I know it must be hard for you," Victoria continued, glancing again at her mobile, probably expecting a call from the saintly Julian making sure she was all right, "but you have to admit, Julian and I have worked hard for everything we have. Nobody handed us anything on a plate."

"I'm not suggesting they did," Jane said, becoming more tense again. She could sense one of her twin's little lectures on life coming on.

"When I was studying all the time at uni, *you* decided to drop out, and when I got the job at the law firm, I was still taking exams while *you* were working on that cruise ship travelling around the world ..."

"Ok, I get the message," Jane interrupted, "and while you were dating the perfect man who would secure your future, I was throwing myself away on all sorts of unreliable types."

"Well, are you coming or not, a week on

Saturday?" Victoria said, signalling for the
bill.

"I already said *no*, but have a good time
anyway."

§

Jane sat on the bus going over the evening
in her mind. No matter how good her
intentions were, and how hard she tried,
lately she always seemed to get off on the
wrong foot with Victoria. It was probably
quite generous of her twin to offer to pay for
a special party, but she just didn't want to be
there. It brought into focus the difference in
their lives -- Victoria's success at anything
she tried, and Jane's own drifting,
unfocused ways: a tiny bedsit in Pimlico she
could hardly afford, a job which consisted of
boringly checking invoices on a computer,
and a part-time boyfriend who fitted her in
between drinks with his colleagues after
work, games of squash, watching (and
endlessly discussing) Arsenal football team,
and going to the gym. He was always
hinting that she should join him in some
sort of exercise, try jogging, or go with him

to the gym, but she just didn't want to expose herself to it. She'd seen those slim, toned, lycra-clad bodies, hair pulled up in a perky ponytail, trendy holdall with yet more expensive trainers and changes of sports clothes inside ... No, she couldn't afford it. She didn't want to join the club; she wouldn't fit in. She wouldn't feel right. She just wanted to try and be happy with herself as she was, a curvy, generous size 16.

She got off the bus and started to walk down the dark, deserted road towards her flat. Deep in thought about the difficult evening, she stepped off the kerb to cross the road, suddenly startled by a squeal of brakes and a flash of black metal as she felt a rush of air which brushed her lightly.

She stepped quickly back onto the pavement, suddenly realising that in her panic she'd dropped her handbag. Stooping down she saw it in the gutter, tangled, ripped and squashed. And as she picked it up she was aware of a loud, throaty roar of noise and saw that the huge, black machine had circled round and was coming *back* towards her. It stopped right next to where she stood, the rider in black leathers towered intimidatingly over her. He took off his crash helmet and leaned down.

"You just stepped straight out in front of me," he said harshly.

"I didn't see you," Jane replied, turning away and gripping her bag tightly to her chest.

"If you're one of those people trying to claim compensation for an injury, forget it," he said.

"I'm not claiming anything, the only thing hurt is my handbag," she said, holding it out for him to see, and suddenly the stress of the whole evening overcame her. To Jane's dismay she felt the tears begin to slide down her face and before she could stop herself, a little sob escaped.

"Oh God, you're crying. Are you hurt? Should you go to hospital?"

"No," she sniffed, trying to wipe her face, scrabbling around in the ragged handbag for a tissue. "I've said I'm okay. Just leave me alone." She was aware of the dark, empty street and the nearness of this tall, overpowering stranger.

"You're shaken," he said, looking around, holding his helmet in one hand and steadying the huge motor cycle with the other. "I passed a pub just down there, let me get you something for the shock."

"It's a very basic place," she replied.

"As long as they have brandy ..."

He was already wheeling the bike towards the pub, and so, trembling slightly, Jane followed him ...

§

He put the glass of brandy in front of her and sat down at the plain wooden table. The pub was quiet, just a few regulars drinking around the bar, two young men playing on the fruit machines, and an elderly man with a mongrel dog, reading a newspaper in the corner.

"Just drink it slowly, take your time," he instructed, watching her carefully as she sipped the fiery liquid.

"I'm okay, honestly. I don't usually cry, it's just that I've had a really crap evening and that sort of finished it off."

"Well, you could tell me all about it? Sometimes it helps to talk to a stranger."

Jane thought about this for a few

moments. It *would* be great to unload her feelings, but was it really fair? The incident had been as much her fault as his. She didn't know anything about him. As if reading her thoughts, he held out his hand.

"Jack Flynn and yes, before you say it, I'm Irish."

Jane took the firm, warm hand, and felt surprisingly comforted.

"Jane Harkness," she offered. She had noticed a slight accent, a lilt in his voice.

She looked at him more closely as he sat opposite her. Brown, curly, slightly long hair, lightly bronzed skin as though he had recently been abroad, the most startlingly blue eyes, with laughter lines crinkling around the edges, firm jawline, and his voice was deep with just a hint of an Irish accent. It was hard to pin him down as far as age was concerned; riding an expensive motor bike, dressed in what must be top of the range leathers, but with a casual, confident air. He could be anybody, maybe late thirties, rich and indulging a hobby or perhaps just an ordinary guy with an interest in motorbikes.

"Well?" he said, relaxing back into his

seat, drinking his beer, obviously happy to listen.

Haltingly at first, not wishing to sound disloyal, Jane told him about the meeting with her twin, Victoria. How it always turned out badly lately whenever they got together, the birthday party arrangements and her refusal to go. She stopped for breath and looked up at Jack Flynn, feeling she had gone on for far too long. How could he possibly be interested in her feelings of inadequacy whenever she was with her twin?

"Was it always competitive between you, even when you were small?" he asked.

"No, not at all," she replied. "We were so close when we were young, just as identical twins usually are. Then, as we got older, things changed, we weren't the cute twins any longer. It all seemed to split into two halves."

"Victoria was cleverer and more studious. She stayed at uni and got a first while I dropped out. She has everything now: a husband, beautiful house, well paid job and just to complete the picture they're having a baby. I even get mad about our *names*.

She's always elegant Victoria, never shortened to Vicky or anything, while I'm just Jane. *Plain* Jane."

"And when did you lose confidence in yourself?"

It was a surprising question, more intimate than she had expected, and for a moment, Jane was completely at a loss. However, she thought carefully and realised that yes, he'd put his finger right on the heart of the problem.

"Actually, it was when we reached our teens," she said. "Victoria transformed into a pretty, bright, poised, grown up girl and I just got all the teenage downsides – spots, shyness, puppy fat, which was supposed to go away and never did. Oh, I've never admitted this to anyone else before ... She has everything in life, and I suppose I'm jealous."

"Understandable."

He seemed to sum up the situation simply, with just one word.

It may have been the brandy or the fact that those piercing blue eyes were on her, but Jane began to relax and enjoy being with Jack Flynn. The hurt of the previous few hours was fading. She looked up and met his steady gaze.

"Sorry to be such a pain and going on. I don't usually, but thanks anyway for listening."

"Sorry I killed your bag."

Jane laughed, it was such a relief to be with someone with a sense of humour.

"So", he asked, "what *are* you going to do for your birthday ... A week on Saturday, did you say?"

Jane shrugged. "I don't honestly have any plans. At the moment I feel it would just be great to get away for the day, out of London, do my own thing."

"No boyfriend to whisk you away somewhere romantic?"

"No-one serious, and if he actually remembers that it's my birthday, he'll probably turn up with a bunch of flowers from a garage, and a box of chocolates."

"So," he asked, "what would your own thing be?"

Jane considered this for a few moments. The sort of day she would like would be far too expensive. She felt that she would like to have time somewhere tranquil to relax and consider her life. Thirty felt like a bit of a milestone. She wanted to think about how she could improve her looks, regain some confidence in herself. But how could she put this into words for this attractive stranger without sounding like a complete loser?

"Oh, maybe just a health spa for the day? Try to get motivated to do something about myself," she eventually said, keeping it short.

"Well, don't get hooked on all that weight loss rubbish," he smiled. "You're good as you are."

Jane was a little surprised at the comment but also pleased. She always felt a little uneasy about her body – if only she could lose a few pounds, be a little more toned and relaxed about her shape – but he had complimented her.

Her night immediately went up a notch.

"If you're totally free on that Saturday, can I make a suggestion?"

Jane nodded, wondering what was coming next.

"I know someone who has a luxury spa hotel just outside Oxford. It has everything: fantastic grounds, beauty treatments as well as the usual pool, sauna and so on. Because it's a fairly new investment they sometimes want an anonymous volunteer to spend a day and try out the services. All that's needed afterwards it to write a short but honest report, you know, the different treatments available and about their experience on the day ... You wouldn't be spying on the staff or anything. It's just about the facilities and if they could be improved."

"I couldn't do that!" she laughed. "I've never been to one of those places in my life. I wouldn't have anything to go on, and anyway why would you offer this to me?"

Jack leaned forward, reached over and put her mangled handbag on the table between them.

"Firstly, because I think I owe you a new handbag and I don't have a clue how to replace it. And secondly, you're just the sort of person to test out this Spa, as you have no preconceptions, so you can be completely honest. How about it?"

Jane started thinking about the great possibility – a *free* day at a beauty spa? Who would turn that down? And it would be a perfect way of getting out of the birthday party, too. She could say, with complete honesty, that she was going to be away for the day. However, there was still the problem of getting there.

"Where did you say it was?" she asked.

"In the country, just this side of Oxford. Not too far."

"I'd have to find out about trains or buses," she said. "I don't have a car."

There seemed to be more problems arising with this idea, but even so she was becoming more and more excited at the prospect.

"Right, it's not costing anything for the day, so I'll arrange a mini cab to take you there and get you back. That will save me the problem of replacing the bag."

Jack spoke firmly, as if used to making arrangements for perfect strangers.

"You *really* mean this? I don't expect anything from you. I think I probably stepped into the road without looking," Jane replied.

"And I was probably going a bit over the speed limit. Give me your mobile number and I'll call you later in the week. That way you can have time to think about it, no pressure, make up your own mind ..."

CHAPTER TWO

Jane stood before the mirror in her tiny bedroom, trying to decide what to wear. Black jeans were fine, but she couldn't decide what to put with them. A jumper – it was Autumn after all – or perhaps a loose blouse and a jacket. And what about when she got there? She wondered if she was expected to take a wrap or dressing gown of some sort, or would it be provided? She decided to pack a swim suit (it looked a little shabby but would have to do), and what about soft shoes - trainers, she thought. It all seemed a little unreal.

She had been pleasantly surprised and

excited when Jack Flynn called her on the Thursday before and confirmed that all the arrangements had been made. A mini cab would call for her at 9.30am to take her to the spa on the Saturday morning and she would be collected at 7.00pm. He reminded her to take a small notebook and make reminders during the day so that she could write up her experiences later. It made the whole thing feel as though she was doing a proper research job and not just accepting a favour. He was very business-like and organised telling her the arrangements, but finished up on a friendly note.

"Well, enjoy your day, Jane, and don't even think about that birthday party," he said.

"Thanks again," she replied. "The thought of getting away from it all is just so great."

She'd made up her mind to take full advantage of this wonderful chance, immerse herself in the day, on her own, doing exactly as she pleased, and having time to think about her future.

§

Greg had been rather quiet when she met him in the wine bar on the Friday night, and she wondered whether he'd somehow learned about the double birthday party – the one which he hadn't been invited to. She didn't know whether to mention it to him, but in the end decided not to. It would only arouse yet more complications, and she didn't want to tell him what she *actually* had planned for the next day. She limited herself to one glass of wine, saying she had a bit of a headache coming on. But really, she wanted to get home, have an early night, in order to feel her best for tomorrow.

As Greg went to the bar to get himself another drink, she watched him with a new feeling of detachment - chinos, dark casual jacket, closely cut fair hair, athletic build, just becoming a little chunky in spite of his regular visits to the gym. They had been seeing each other for over a year, but Jane never felt she really knew his deeper thoughts – if he even had any. In her heart she knew that the relationship wasn't going anywhere; it had just become a convenience, someone to see, to hang out with, a matter of routine for both of them.

"You're a bit quiet," she said when he returned with his own lager.

"Oh, it's just work," she said. "There's talk of cutting down, I might start to have a look round for something."

"I'm sure you'll be okay. You might find something better anyway."

Greg was in I.T. and had appeared settled in his job, but from time to time he became restless, wanting to get on, and complaining that he was under-paid.

"Do you want us to go early?" Greg was draining his glass rather quickly and Jane knew he thought he was going to stay the night with her.

"Actually," she said, "I think this might be a migraine coming on. I'll just go and have an early night ..."

She wanted to be back in her little flat, getting ready and anticipating the exciting next day.

"There's a match tomorrow afternoon, so I'll see you later," Greg murmured, getting to his feet.

There had been no mention of her birthday and Jane realised that he had probably forgotten it, or perhaps might make some token effort the next day.

"I won't be there," she said, deciding to get it out of the way. "I'm away for the day."

"What about later in the evening then?" he said. But he was still too preoccupied with his own thoughts; he really wasn't getting the message.

Jane felt annoyed. Thirty was a special birthday and he had obviously been too busy thinking about the wretched football match with his mates and his own problems to give her any thought whatsoever!

"No, I might not be back until late," she said. "Let's just leave it."

Then she put her coat on and grabbed her bag, walking towards the door.

§

Saturday, her 30th birthday! She had received a few cards from the girls at work and put them up in the little, crowded sitting room. The post wouldn't come until after she'd left, and she guessed that most people would take them to the party in the evening, thinking that she would be there.

She had heard nothing more from Victoria in the two weeks since their meal. She probably still thought that Jane would change her mind and turn up. How wrong she was. For a moment Jane felt mean about her parents and grandparents who would all be expecting to see her, then she visualised the great announcement, all the focus on Victoria and her news. She admitted to herself that she just couldn't face it -- being second place again.

She was ready well before the mini cab was due and spent the time fixing her make up. If she took her time with it, she knew she could make the most of her pale complexion and hazel eyes. She brushed her shoulder-length red hair, wishing it was straight and glossy instead of thick and wavy, and blonde instead of red.

She began to feel excited. It had been such a long time since she had a day to indulge herself and she meant to make the most of it. It might feel strange being on her own instead of sharing with a girl friend, but it would give her space and time to think and relax. Best of all, it had been arranged by that charismatic Irishman, Jack Flynn, and maybe she would see him again once she'd written her report about the day.

The thought was certainly thrilling.

It was some time since she had met anyone so relaxed and confident, but, at the same time he appeared to be totally unaware of his devastating looks and sex appeal. Just friendly and focused, with no silly chat up lines, but she was intrigued and wished she could know more about him.

§

The double wrought-iron gates stood open and the cab turned into the gravelled drive. Jane looked out of the window at the expanse of grass and trees on the right hand side and the large, dark lake shimmering on the left. The drive continued, bordered by tall trees, eventually stopping at the entrance to an imposing country house. The driver opened the door and Jane thanked him. It seemed that the fare was all arranged. She went up the stone steps, through glass doors, into the impressive entrance hall. The floor was marble, the huge reception desk in glossy walnut wood, with magnificent fresh flower arrangements on either side. She glanced at the receptionist: a pretty, blonde girl in an expensive silver-grey suit with a dazzling white blouse.

"Jane Harkness," she introduced herself, suddenly nervous, hoping that this dream day had all been properly booked and arranged and that nothing was going to go wrong.

"Oh, yes, Miss Harkness, could I just ask you to sign the register and I'll get the key."

"Key? I'm only here for the day, I didn't expect a room," Jane said, flustered.

"That's all right! As you're here for the whole day, we've given you one of the quiet rooms to yourself, just to rest if you want. There's a single bed, en suite, flowers and magazines and it overlooks the lake. Some of our more exclusive guests just come for peace and quiet – a walk in the grounds, a swim and a read – so we like to provide them with their own space."

Jane was amazed. She hadn't expected anything like this. It must be really top of the range.

The receptionist passed her a key – Room

12 – and a leaflet.

"This should give you the details of all our facilities: pool, spa, sauna, massages, beauty treatments. Just have a look through and if you want any of the special treatments contact Reception and we'll work out a timetable for you. Is there anything else I can help you with?" she said politely.

"I don't think so," Jane replied.

"Oh, and you can order any food from the menu in your room at lunchtime, if you want, and there is a buffet and wine in the main restaurant from six o'clock."

It just got better and better! Jane had felt slightly uneasy at the thought of eating on her own, and here it had been solved - she could order room service at lunch time and plan her day around that.

§

Room 12 was spacious and tranquil, situated at the side of the hotel, overlooking the lake. It was decorated in soothing shades of white and pale green, had a single bed with mounds of cushions, a large coffee table with paperback books and glossy magazines, fresh flowers and a bowl of fruit. A green velvet sofa by the window faced the lake and the extensive, sweeping grounds. There was no TV or radio, just a white telephone and an expensive-looking brochure detailing the delights of the Spa. Jane explored the huge en-suite, which was tiled entirely in pale grey marble. As well as a walk-in power shower, there was a white roll-top bath, exclusive bath gels, oils and creams, heaps of folded, thick white towels and a white robe and slippers. The mini-fridge in the bedroom held choices of fruit juices and mineral water – but no alcohol!

Switching her mobile off, Jane sat on the sofa and felt herself melt into the background. A whole free day of luxurious relaxation. Her 30th birthday, a day to do whatever she wanted, with no-one to interfere or make arrangements on her behalf. No well-meaning advice that she didn't want. No phone calls, no Greg taking her for granted, but wanting a quick sex session later. How on earth had Jack arranged it all. She read lazily through the leaflet and decided on a plan. A dip in the pool first, as swimming had always been the only form of exercise she really enjoyed. This could be followed by any water treatments available – sauna, spa, and so on – then a walk in the grounds, followed by a lazy lunch in her room. She saw that she needed to order from a range of healthy options. If she wanted she could lie on the soft bed and read the beauty magazines, get some idea of new fashions and styles, and get motivated to try and change her image. And afterwards, if she fell into a light snooze, what did it matter? And for the afternoon, she decided to try out some massage treatments, then the beauty facilities – facial, pedicure and hair do.

She'd see how she felt about the buffet at the end; she might just want to relax in her room. She wasn't sure about joining other people. She had the feeling that they might all be slim, elegant, beautifully dressed model types and she would feel out of place. It would depend on how the day went.

She became aware that she should be making some notes as she went along, but decided to catch up later. The fabulous day was just beginning ...

CHAPTER THREE

Everything went perfectly. Jane had forgotten just how much she enjoyed swimming, and happily ploughed up and down the water in the warm, sapphire coloured pool, which she had almost to herself. Next she tried the jacuzzi and sauna, then, wrapped in the thick, white robe, went back to her room. She soaked contentedly in the bath, pouring in heaps of expensive oils. A power shower followed as she indulged herself with the expensive shower gels and body lotions. She wanted to try out everything in the bathroom, like a child in a sweetshop.

When she was eventually dressed, she looked out of the window at the lake. The day was slightly sunny and the sky bright blue. She felt energised and decided to explore the extensive grounds. As she walked, she began to feel even more invigorated. She looped around the lake and took a path right out to the edge of the estate, walking further than she had intended.

Back in her room, after the walk, she felt hungry and ordered fresh salmon salad and fruit from the room service menu. She would've liked a glass of wine with it, too, but resisted. She wanted to make the most of this healthy day and not feel too drowsy later. As she waited for the room service, she poured a glass of apple juice from mini fridge and sat looking out over the lake.

This birthday was totally different from any other. How had Jack Flynn managed it, she wondered. It was so obviously ultra-expensive, and she hoped that he really *did* know the owner and wasn't just treating her to this day because he felt guilty for nearly knocking her over and ruining her best handbag.

It had been such a long time since she'd
actually had time completely to herself and
the space and inclination to think about her
future. She knew in her heart that she was
envious of Victoria, who had, admittedly,
worked very hard for her achievements, but
still seemed to have everything she wanted
in life. Julian – a model husband, hard-
working and considerate – although, if she
really thought deeply, it seemed to Jane that
he was a bit of a bland geek. He wouldn't do
for her; no, she liked men with more spark,
more depth.

Then there was Victoria and Julian's
house: all very minimal and labour saving,
but how would a crawling, time consuming
baby fit in?

Finally, of course, Victoria herself; a
successful career woman, but she would
either have to suspend her career for while
to stay at home or find help with the baby if
she wanted to continue working.

As Jane considered all these problems,
she found herself thinking that perhaps life
wasn't quite as easy for Victoria as she had
thought. Anyway, it was time to consider her
own future – she really must take some

positive steps, and start to look for another job. Even if she didn't find something which paid more, at least she might find a more interesting way of earning her money. She would have to continue living in her tiny bedsit, but she could do something about her personal life.

This brought her back to the question of Greg. She had a distinct feeling that she was just letting the relationship drift on because they had dropped into a familiar routine. She felt used when he spent so much time with his mates watching football or going to the gym, just turning up when he was ready to spend the night.

When was the last time he had surprised her with a present, just a little gift, or even a night out somewhere other than the pub?

If Jane really looked closely at their relationship, she knew it wasn't going anywhere. She would make up her mind on at least one definite change in her life.

Greg would have to go.

She felt that this day away had given her the time to think and make the decision, and surprised herself at how much better she felt. She had been coasting, putting decisions off, and now it was time for a new start.

§

After lunch, she had booked appointments for the afternoon, starting with an aromatherapy body massage, head massage, facial, pedicure and, lastly a cut and blow dry. The assistants were all friendly but professional, and, if she had been a little embarrassed at first about revealing her ample curves, she soon relaxed under their expert care. It was so soothing. She drifted, thinking carefully about her life – it was time to make some big changes and the day was just giving her time to gather her thoughts.

"It's great here isn't it?" the woman next to her in the pedicure seats said.

"Oh yes, I'm really enjoying it," Jane replied.

She glanced across to see a middle-aged woman wrapped in a white robe, with grey stylish hair, brown eyes and a kind smile.

It was good to speak to another of the guests, and here was someone quite ordinary looking, not some gorgeous, leggy model type, and obviously having a good time.

"I come twice a year - it's my little treat to myself," the woman said.

"For the day?" Jane asked.

"No, the weekend. I always ask for vouchers for Christmas and my birthday, then I save up the rest and come in the Spring and Autumn. Get away from the family, for a change," she laughed.

"What a great idea," Jane replied. She didn't mention that it was actually her own birthday; she just wanted to keep the conversation casual.

"They seem to manage without me, and just occasionally I like my own space, to be spoiled."

Jane knew just how she felt, and they fell into an easy chat as Laura told Jane about her family – two teenagers who kept her running round all the time and a husband devoted to his allotment. Laura said that she would be going down to the buffet at six, if Jane wanted to join her.

She accepted readily, as Laura was easy company, and it meant that she wouldn't be eating on her own. It would be a good end to the perfect, heavenly day.

"Don't expect filling food," Laura warned. "It's all delicate, healthy options, but very tasty."

Too soon, the experience was coming to an end – the facial, and finally the hair salon. Jane was pleased when she saw herself in the mirror: she looked relaxed, with a healthy colour in her cheeks, and her hair fell easily into a new and very different sleek, layered cut.

She met Laura in the restaurant and filled her plate with the small buffet items, plus a glass of white wine. They seated themselves at a small side table, and Jane thought it was time she remembered why she was there.

"So, have you been here many times then?" she asked. "Everything appears to be new?"

"Oh I've been coming for the last few years," said Laura. "About a year ago, it was taken over by some French consortium, and they must have poured money into it, improved it no end. The whole place has been re-styled, it's much more up-market.

Of course, as you know, it's *very* expensive."

Jane agreed politely. She didn't want to reveal that she hadn't a clue what it all cost and that she was supposed to be reviewing the Spa. She wished that she was staying for the weekend, for another day of pampering, and Laura seemed so friendly, it had all gone far too quickly. She made a resolution to come again, save up for a treat.

After a while she looked at her watch. It was nearly seven, and the mini cab would be calling for her. She felt like Cinderella having to leave the ball before midnight. She said goodbye to Laura, collected her things, and took the room key back to Reception.

"I think there may be a cab coming for me, I'll just wait here," she said, turning slowly towards the large glass doors, just in time to see them opening and Jack Flynn walking through. Jack, dressed in his black leathers, crash helmet in one hand and a bag in the other.

He looked at her with a wide grin, and something flickered in his eyes – was it appreciation, desire even? Jane wasn't sure.

"Your transport awaits," he said.

CHAPTER FOUR

"A *motor bike*?"

Jane's reactions were all over the place – she was amazed and pleased to see Jack, then completely astounded that he wanted to take her back to London on his bike.

He was smiling at her, reading her body language.

"You should do one more exciting, new thing on your birthday," he said. "And I promise you I'll take it really easy. After 25 miles we'll stop and if you don't like it, then I'll put you in a taxi."

They were standing next to the huge, black machine. In the bag he had a leather jacket and helmet for her.

"What if they don't fit me?" She was stalling for time, unable to make up her mind whether she was excited or just scared stiff.

"Oh, they will. Have you never been a pillion passenger before?"

Jane shook her head. Not only had she never been on a motor bike, but she was also reluctant to spoil her fabulous new hairstyle by cramming it under a heavy crash helmet.

"Happy birthday, by the way."

"Thank you," she replied. "And thanks also for arranging the day - it was wonderful."

"Right," he said, handing her the leather jacket. "Put this on. All you have to remember is that you lean with the bike when we go around a bend, not against it. Left bend, lean left, okay?"

Jane nodded. How could she resist? She was beginning to feel a tremor of something, unsure if it was fear, or perhaps the exciting idea of sitting behind Jack, clutching him tightly all the way back to London.

He leaned down and adjusted the helmet so that it felt snug, and as he did, his fingers brushed her face.

"You smell lovely, by the way," he murmured unexpectedly.

Jane took a deep breath as he got onto the bike and steadied it.

"Up you get ..."

§

Jack was right. After the first few minutes, when she just held on fearfully with her eyes closed, Jane actually did begin to get used to the ride – the vibration of the powerful engine, the throaty noise, and the air rushing past. The country lanes were almost deserted and it was just getting dusk as they made their way towards the capital. She was aware of his lean, hard body beneath the protective gear and enjoyed the sensation of holding onto him. Before long they were coming into a small town, and she had lost all track of her whereabouts, as he pulled slowly into a lay-by and stopped.

He turned towards her and raised his voice. "We'll be hitting more traffic soon.

Do you want to go on, or a taxi? Your choice."

Jane nodded. She *did* want to continue, to her amazement, and she felt she could ride all night with Jack.

"Is there anything else you want?" he asked. "I can stop on the way?"

Before she'd even thought about it, Jane said that she was hungry and Jack shouted with laughter.

"Didn't you eat at the restaurant?"

He was still smiling at her and she wished that she had kept her mouth shut. He would think she was obsessed with food.

"I did," she said, "but it was all so light and I had such an appetite, it must have been all the swimming and walking." She felt that she had to explain her hunger.

"Leave it with me," he said, revving up the engine and just like that they were back on the road.

§

They were coming into the city now. More traffic, lights in the shop windows, Saturday night groups of people out for the evening.

Jane tried to work out where they were but it was all just a blur. Jack left the busy road and began to weave into a quieter area. He stopped the bike and turned off the engine, then loosened his helmet. Jane looked around and saw that they were outside a small fish and chip shop. He helped her down and then parked the bike.

"The best fish and chips in London, and there's a little cafe at the back," he said as she followed him through.

There was a small room with tables set out, and he took off his crash helmet, then the leather jacket and hung it over a spare chair and sat down. Jane did the same and ran her hand through her tumbled hair, wondering if anything remained of the new style.

She began to wonder what this crazy day had in store for her next. Here she was in a chip shop, ravenous and ready to eat anything, after the most luxurious, up market, pampering day she had ever experienced – it was such a contrast!

She looked up to see him watching her closely.

"You coped really well with that, for your

first ride," he said.

"I enjoyed it," she replied. "It was a bit scary at first, but great. I feel as though this is the most exciting, unexpected birthday I've ever had."

"*Two* things you've never done before – the Spa and the motor bike. So? How do you rate them?"

He was teasing her, waiting for her reaction.

"Both completely different and exciting," she said. "I don't know how long it's been since I had such fun."

He leaned forward and took her hand in his.

"Don't lose your enthusiasm for life, Jane. It's very appealing."

"Well, without you I'd be stuck at a family gathering, taking second place, as usual," she said.

"And did they miss you at the party?" he asked.

"I don't know, I turned my phone off. I'm sure there'll be lots of messages, but I'll look at them later."

Jack went up to the counter to place their order and came back with two mugs of tea.

Jane sipped hers slowly; she didn't want to rush anything. She wanted this night to go on, and there was only an empty bedsit to go back to.

"What sort of bike is it?" she asked, knowing nothing at all about them.

"A Harley Davidson Electra Glide, customised, and my other is a Ducati, an Italian make."

"*Two* bikes, or do you have more?" she asked.

"Just the two, at the moment. It's a bit of a hobby of mine."

The plates of fish and chips appeared, and Jane ate the delicious food hungrily. *Forget the calories*, she thought, *just enjoy the moment.*

"So, did you learn enough to write a nice, long report?" Jack had finished by now, and leaned back casually in his chair as he spoke.

"Oh yes, the whole thing was absolutely great, but I've made notes and I'll write it up in detail. Does your friend want it soon?"

"I think around a week or so will be fine."

"And did you have time to think about yourself? What you want in life?" He was looking deeply into her eyes now, and Jane felt that, for some reason, she could really talk to this man, who was still almost a stranger.

"I've decided to look for a more interesting job and not give up," she said, "no matter how long it takes. Also, I'm going to finish with Greg. I don't want to be taken for granted anymore."

"Well, think carefully, don't do anything rash," he said softly, his Irish brogue more pronounced.

"Oh, it's been coming for a while," she replied. "I just needed the time and space to think about it and make sure." She felt calm as she spoke; she had made her mind up and it was good to finally put it into words.

Just then, Jane realised that she still knew next to nothing about this handsome Irishman seated opposite her. He knew the best fish and chip shop in London and appeared quite relaxed there, but he also knew about the most expensive spa hotel around and drove motor bikes obviously worth thousands of pounds.

Who was he?

She tried to curb her curiosity, but sensed

that he was aware of her struggle, and somehow he seemed to be able to read her mind.

"I live in London," he offered, "near the river for some of the year. I have business interests in France, too, so I spend most of the time there."

"I don't want to seem nosy," Jane said, looking away, a little embarrassed that she'd been so transparent.

"I keep the motor bikes in this country. I'm a bit of a speed fanatic, and I prefer to drive on the left." He shrugged. "Horses, that's my main interest. Breeding, training, racing. But obviously not in London, which is why I'm mostly in France."

Married, separated, divorced, single? She wanted to ask so many more questions, but knew she must restrain herself. This man had given her the best birthday she could have hoped for and she wasn't going to spoil it now.

Too soon they'd finished their meals and then Jack rose, gathering both jackets from the spare chair.

"Time to go," he said. "You must give me directions so I can drop you off."

So Jane gave him instructions and they got back onto the bike. She wanted the evening to carry on, for this magical day to last a little longer. She thought about asking him in for coffee, but felt unsure. Would he think she was trying to push their friendship? Or did he feel the tension of her own growing attraction?

She felt flustered.

Better to say goodnight casually, she decided. And she would have to contact him again when she had done the report; perhaps then they might have another meeting then.

They pulled up outside her address, and he helped her from the bike. She handed him the extra jacket and crash helmet, which he stowed in a pannier on the back.

"Goodnight birthday girl," he said, leaning down and gently kissing her cheek.

Jane enjoyed the moment, leaning slightly against him, lingering, wishing it was more than just a birthday kiss.

"Thank you again," she said. "Today was fabulous."

When she got back to her flat she turned on her phone and checked her messages. A short text from Victoria saying happy birthday, nothing more, she was obviously put out at Jane's absence.

There were messages from the rest of the family, too, wondering why she hadn't gone to the party.

She made up her mind that she would go and visit her parents the following day, have Sunday lunch with them and try to mend the situation. She had to think of a plausible reason why she'd turned down the invitation. Perhaps they all thought that she was offended because Greg hadn't been invited. It *was* a possible excuse, but she didn't think she should use him in that way.

She kicked off her shoes and then lay back on her single bed. She just wanted to go over the whole day again in her mind, re-live it all: the spa hotel, the treatments, the feeling that she was about to make some changes in her life.

And, best of all, Jack Flynn, the mysterious biker that she had got to know a little better. She would make sure that she wrote up a really professional report on the hotel, then she would be ready when he contacted her in about a week. She imagined handing it over to him in some small, intimate wine bar, sitting close, reading it together, then perhaps she would ask him back for coffee, and after that? Jack in her flat, Jack holding her, kissing her, moving her slowly towards the bedroom. She closed her eyes and let her imagination go wild ...

§

Jane was awakened in the morning by the sound of hammering on her door. She rolled sleepily out of bed, grabbed a towelling robe and thrust her feet into her old, worn slippers. She opened the door and was greeted by the sight of Greg in his running gear. He pushed roughly past her and then stood there in the middle of the small room.

"I came round last night. Where were you?" he asked.

"Last night? I told you I wasn't going to be here." Jane was annoyed that he felt he could come round and question her just because she hadn't been available when he happened to drop in.

"I asked where you *where*?" Greg repeated, and Jane wondered if there was an undertone of jealousy in his voice. Well it would serve him right.

"I went to a health spa for the day," she said. "Out of London, and didn't get back until late."

"What on earth for? You'll never come to the gym with me, and I'm always asking you." He sounded like a spoilt little boy who was not getting his own way.

"If you ever bothered to listen you'd know that I don't want to go to the gym or pound the streets jogging. This was a relaxation and beauty weekend and I treated myself to it for my birthday."

Jane could tell from his face that she'd caught him on the hop. He had obviously forgotten all about her birthday.

"Your birthday?" he asked. "Yesterday?"

"Yes," she replied, "and before you say that I should've reminded you, let's just get this out of the way. I don't really care one way or the other about presents and cards and so on. What I care about is that it just shows how shallow our relationship is. You do your thing and expect me to be here whenever you fancy a quickie or a bed for the night. Well, now that I've reached the age of thirty, I've decided that it isn't enough. It's over Greg. We can be friends if you like, but nothing more." At this, Jane stopped, breathless, surprised that she had managed to get it all out in one go.

For a moment Greg appeared to be lost for words. He paced the tiny room shaking his head, filling the space between them with waves of anger and disbelief.

"Just like that, after over a year?" he glared. "Well, don't think that one day at a health spa is going to transform you. You'll still be overweight and dull. Take a look at your twin sometime, and see how you *could* look."

It was cruel and Jane was shocked that he should be quite so hurtful. She tried to regain her composure and hold back her shock at his cruel words. She didn't like scenes and had hoped that this break up could have been done in a more civilised manner.

"Just *go*, Greg," she said, "and don't come back."

After he had stormed out, she collapsed

onto the sofa. His words had been wounding, but at least she knew she had done the right thing in finishing it with him. She'd be much better off without him in her life, but even so, she still felt bruised. She just needed to get some confidence in herself, and come to terms with her body shape and her looks – try to accept herself.

Out of the blue she recalled the night before, when Jack had brushed her cheek with his hand and told her that she smelled lovely.

That was the sort of man she wanted.

It may be an impossible dream, but she knew in her heart that she deserved someone better than Greg. Someone who would love her for herself and not use her, or try to change her.

This was going to be a new beginning, she decided. But first she had to face the family.

CHAPTER FIVE

"You can peel the carrots and cut them up."

Jane was in the kitchen with her mother. At first, when she rang and suggested visiting for Sunday lunch, Marion had been a little cool.

"Where *were* you last night? We were expecting you at the party," she'd said.

"A previous arrangement," Jane had explained. "I'll tell you all about it when I see you ..."

Jane chopped the carrots and leaned on the kitchen table watching her mother whisk the batter for her famous Yorkshire puddings. She took a deep breath and decided that she must get the party question out of the way, once and for all.

"Someone I know had arranged a full day at a beauty spa, as a special birthday treat. They went to a lot of trouble and expense. So I couldn't just drop out when Victoria suddenly sprang the idea of the party. She didn't let me know in time."

There was a small silence while her mother thought this over.

"Oh, I see, we did all wonder what had happened." Marion seemed to be unbending a little.

"And, before you ask about Greg," Jane continued, "I must tell you that it's over."

"What a shame to happen around your birthday," Marion sighed.

Jane could tell that although her mother had never been keen on Greg, she wanted to ask more about the break up. But Jane was determined not to go into detail; it was over, that was enough.

"It wasn't going anywhere, so it's better this way," Jane said. She felt that she had got all the tricky questions out of the way.

Her mother put the carrots on to steam and turned towards Jane.

"Your hair looks nice. You've changed your style."

And at that, Jane was happy to tell her all about the various treatments she'd tried at the Spa and the beauty salon.

She just wanted to have a relaxing Sunday lunch and a glass of wine. Later she would make a start on her report, draft out some ideas.

"Victoria and Julian are coming to eat," Marion added. "I thought it would save her having to cook. What do you think about the news?"

"Great," Jane answered. "And you must be looking forward to being a granny."

§

They sat around the large dining table. Her father, Alan, relaxed, opening the wine, telling jokes and passing the vegetables. Julian was looking especially pleased with himself and mentioned finding a decorator to get the nursery ready in plenty of time. Victoria, dressed in an elegant, jersey shift dress was talking about maternity leave. She'd not mentioned anything about Jane not turning up at the party, so perhaps she was to be forgiven.

Jane sat quietly and looked around. *It could be worse*, she thought. At least they were a family that could get together for a meal without too much tension.

The Sunday dinner was delicious, tender roast beef, Yorkshire pudding and roast potatoes, loads of fresh vegetables. She smiled to herself as she heaped her plate, remembering the fish and chips the night before and her exhilarating ride on the powerful motorbike. She imagined bringing Jack Flynn to one of her mother's family meals and knew that Marion would be absolutely charmed by him.

Jane became aware that Victoria was silently picking at her food, and suddenly she pushed back her chair and rushed out of the room. They all looked over at Julian.

"Morning sickness," he explained sheepishly.

"Morning? It's one o'clock!" Alan commented.

"It comes on at any time of the day."

Jane realised that Marion was on edge, wondering whether to go after Victoria or stay at the table. After a time Victoria returned, pale and shaky looking, her usually immaculate hair damp and plastered to her forehead. She sat back at her place but pushed her plate away, sipping slowly from a glass of water. Jane had never seen her twin quite so unsettled for years, and unexpectedly felt a sudden wave of sympathy.

"Victoria," she said, "I was telling Mum that I've broken up with Greg." She was hoping cause a distraction. "Because he's an arse," she added, deciding to be truthful, and the table exploded with laughter.

She felt better – better that she was becoming more assertive, and speaking her mind. It was a new sensation for Jane and she liked it.

§

Later that afternoon, Julian and Alan took the dog for a walk, their mother was reading the Sunday newspapers, and Victoria and Jane had gone up to the large bedroom they'd shared as children. It was a substantial, family house and they could have had a bedroom each, but the two had always wanted to be together when they were young. The room was still decorated just as it had been when they were teenagers: same curtains and duvet covers, same posters on the wall. Somehow it was comforting. Victoria opened one of the cupboards and was taking out part of her old collection of cuddly toys.

"Look, they're still in such good condition!" she exclaimed. "I'd kind of forgotten about some of them."

"You always took care of your things," Jane said, lying back contentedly on the bed which had belonged once to her, full of wine and heavenly food.

Victoria placed the toys in neat rows on her own bed.

"Do you really not mind about Greg?" she asked. "You know, about breaking up?"

"Definitely not," Jane replied. "It was my decision, something I should have done ages ago,"

Victoria sat on the opposite bed, still a little fragile looking, and glanced at her twin.

"Whatever they did at that Spa, it seems

to have had a good effect on you," she said. "You're different somehow."

Jane smiled. "I'm just taking control of my life for a change."

To her surprise, Victoria appeared upset.

"Just when I seem to be losing it," she said quietly.

"What on earth do you mean? You have *everything*, and the icing on the cake will be the baby!"

"I know all that," Victoria sighed, picking up a pillow and clutching it tightly to her.

"You were fine the other week when we met," Jane added, "and what about the party that you organised? It sounds like it was a great success."

Jane was surprised to see her twin so unsettled.

"Oh, I've just felt so wretched with this sickness. It comes on any time and the last few days have been absolutely terrible. I don't really know how I got through the party yesterday."

Jane was astonished, but decided to keep quiet; perhaps Victoria needed a shoulder to cry on, for a change.

"To make it worse, Julian doesn't

understand. He's read that morning sickness will usually go away after the first three months, and he expects life to be like a text book. I'm just tired all the time, and work is really draining, but I have to keep up, and when I get home, well ..."

"He doesn't help?" Jane was careful, treading cautiously, and this was the first time she had ever heard about even the slightest dent in Julian's halo, or his perfection as a husband. She didn't want to push for information, although she was dying to hear more.

"He's full of ideas for having the nursery decorated and the garden landscaped so it's safe for a toddler, and I'm too tired to care. And he isn't that sympathetic when I'm queasy, either. He likes people to be healthy, so he doesn't deal with illness very well. Then, and don't repeat this or I'll kill you, he's very demanding in bed and I'm just too exhausted to be interested."

Jane put her hands over her face. This was just too much to take in. She began to think that although her own life was a bit dull; it wasn't too bad compared with Victoria's at the moment. It was a revelation, and totally unexpected.

"Couldn't you take some time off work, and just rest a bit?" Jane offered. It was all she could come up with.

"Oh, I'll have to wait for maternity leave," Victoria said. She sat up and gathered up the toys, making an effort to pull herself together, probably regretting her confessions. "Forget what I said, I'm just a bit low."

§

When she got home, Jane took out the notes she had made about the Spa and read them through. She was still stunned by Victoria's revelations, and she wanted to go round and punch that idiot Julian on the nose. Perhaps it could be part of her new assertive attitude, she thought. She dragged herself back to her notes and began to expand them, going over the day, re-visiting each treatment and experience. It had all been so enjoyable, she decided that she would try and save up to go again. She could be like Laura, the woman she'd met there, who went twice a year.

And then her thoughts turned to the eventual end of the day, walking to Reception and seeing Jack coming towards her, and her surprise and delight in seeing him. She was looking forward to giving this report to him; she wanted to see him again and, if possible, she wanted to get to know more about him.

During the following week, Jane polished what she had written, put it onto a memory stick and took it into work, to print out two copies during her lunch hour. She was pleased with the result. It was quite professional looking, and she allowed herself to daydream about a perfect job where she went round the country trying out luxurious spas and hotels and writing up about them. Jack had not given her his e-mail address and she wondered if he had wanted hard copies of the report so they could go over it together – sorting out any queries, and perhaps getting to know each other a little more.

She was hoping that he would ring towards the end of the week and suggest meeting to hand over the report ...

§

Jane glanced around the small apartment. It looked shabby and she decided on a complete clean. It might be that Jack called on her unexpectedly, and so she wanted to be ready. She tried to make the tiny space as appealing as possible. A bright tablecloth over the scratched table, new cushions on the sofa, two new china mugs, some expensive coffee, a bottle of decent red wine and a stock of lager in the fridge.

She wandered into the small bedroom and despaired. The furniture had all come with the flat and was old and tired. In a mad rush of optimism, she measured the window and during her lunch break the next day bought new curtains and a jazzy, matching duvet cover.

The room was a little more attractive now, and, with a shiver of excitement, she tried to imagine Jack Flynn stretched out on the bed, his eyes assessing her and his strong hands pulling her down. It was too much, she didn't really know him, or anything much about him, and she was just letting herself get carried away in a fantasy.

Still, spurred on by her efforts with the flat, she treated herself to new, lacy underwear too, and a silky, loose top, which skimmed her curves -- which she could wear with her best black trousers.

She deliberately didn't add up the items that she'd put on her credit card, she would worry about that next month.

The week went by – work, shopping, cleaning – but by the weekend, Jack *still* hadn't contacted her.

The empty days of Saturday and Sunday loomed ahead of her, and every time her phone rang, or a text appeared, she hoped it would be him. Of course, he had only said *about* a week; he hadn't specified any exact time.

Greg sent a text asking if she had come to her senses and wanted to go out on Saturday night. But she ignored it.

On the Saturday, she drifted round the shops in the afternoon, then bought a pasta ready meal and watched a DVD. Later that evening, Greg sent a further text, probably from the pub, which she ignored and deleted, then went to bed early.

Wondering how to fill her time and

feeling restless, she rang Victoria and asked if she could go round at lunchtime on Sunday. For once she actually wanted to visit the perfect house, have a chat with her twin, and see how things were.

§

When Julian opened the door, Jane found it hard to forget Victoria's complaints about him. She was seeing him in a new light now, but he was polite as sat her down with a glass of wine.

"We're just having a light lunch, soup and crusty bread, and a pudding. No Sunday dinner I'm afraid. Is that ok for you?" he asked.

"Fine," she answered, hoping that the pudding might possibly be chocolate brownie with cream. "How're things?"

"Pretty good," he said. "I've managed to find a decorator for the nursery, so we've decided to have a couple more rooms done as well."

Jane looked around – the minimalist interior with its pale walls and modern furniture looked perfect to her. What on earth could a decorator find to do?

Just then, Victoria called from the kitchen that lunch was ready and she followed Julian out to eat at the large kitchen table. She noticed that Victoria still looked pale and there were dark rings beneath her eyes. Her plate contained one slice of wholemeal toast with a small bowl of soup.

Eat for two! Jane wanted to shout, although it was probably the wrong advice, and she managed to restrain herself.

"How's your search for another job going?" Victoria asked.

"Oh, I haven't really started yet," Jane said. In truth, she had forgotten she'd told her twin about trying to change her life; she had been too busy thinking about that elusive Irishman.

"You could go to night school? Try and get some qualifications?"

Jane sipped her delicious red wine. It was an expensive bottle, she could tell, and she enjoyed the richness and texture.

They drifted through lunch with talk of ante-natal classes, cots and nursery designs. Jane felt herself becoming drowsy and had a struggle to keep awake, but she tried to show some interest.

As she listened, she began to re-assess Julian. He totally immersed himself in any new challenge as though his life depended upon it. So, he was highly qualified and even more highly paid, but he would be hard to live with and at the same time boring. Sure, they had a superb, roomy Victorian renovated house and two expensive cars standing outside. Victoria and the baby would have everything of the best, but they would have to put up with this geeky bore, too.

Jane realised that she would rather have Jack Flynn in his leathers any day, or better still *without* them – whether he had money or not.

Julian was just launching into the problems of finding a garden designer when Jane's phone bleeped. She had meant to turn it off whilst they were eating. *Another wretched text from Greg*, she thought, snatching it from her bag. Instead it was from Jack, a simple question: would she be in around seven tonight if he called in on her?

Jane's face flushed and she was sure that they could hear her heart hammering in her chest.

She glanced at her watch. they had been talking for ages and she was amazed to see that it was almost 4 o' clock now.

Nearly an hour on public transport to get home, a scented bath, hair wash and blow dry, clean the tiny bathroom. She wanted to go, to take it slowly getting ready and still have time to try and calm down before Jack arrived.

CHAPTER SIX

The bathroom was filled with the scented steam of expensive bath oils and lotions, the remains of the free samples she had brought from the Spa. Jane soaked in the bath, her eyes closed, letting her body relax. The weekend at the Spa had encouraged her to give herself more time, a slow soak in the bath instead of a quick shower. Images of Jack kept floating into her mind - his concern when he thought he had knocked into her with the motor bike, his surprise appearance at the Spa, his goodnight kiss when he dropped her off. The clock was ticking, and with a tremor of anticipation, she realised that in less than a couple of hours he would be here, in her tiny apartment.

She draped a towel around her and went into her small bedroom. Letting the towel drop, she looked at herself critically in the full length mirror. She had long outgrown the spots that plagued her teenage years and, having made sure that she was oiled and creamed, her skin was soft and smooth. Her hair had fallen nicely into the new layered style and she blow-dried and brushed it into a glossy shape. Next she put drops into her hazel eyes, which were sparkling with anticipation.

She took the new underwear from the packet and put on the lacy pants and bra, a sexy black, more delicate and flimsy than anything she usually wore. It was some time since she had deliberately bought herself such expensive, provocative underwear but she felt down-hearted when she looked at her shape. She was curvy, rounded, slightly over-weight and there was no disguising it. She had never had the willpower to try any real attempt to reduce her weight or indulge in strenuous exercise. Greg had tried to interest her in running and pressured her into going to the gym, but it had never appealed to her.

That was over now, she decided, no more letting anyone try to change her. If there was any possibility that Jack liked her, then this would be the package, just as she stood, for once in her life she wanted a genuine response.

She put on her black trousers and the new, emerald green silky shirt. *Green*, she thought. Had she chosen a colour closely associated with Ireland without thinking? Perhaps it was a lucky omen!

She couldn't remember when she had last felt so churned up, whether from being excited, aroused or nervous she wasn't sure. He was an attractive, unknown and unpredictable man and had opened a new and unexpected door in her life.

Jane took a last look around the bedroom, straightened the bedclothes and dimmed the lights. She remembered that she had some tea lights in the kitchen and found a couple of pretty saucers to put them in. With the new curtains and duvet, and subdued lighting, the room was a little more inviting. Her heart began to race and she tingled, her imagination was running wild.

She tidied the living room, polished a couple of wine glasses and set out and lit candles on the worn coffee table. She switched off the main light and put the table lamp on. Realistically, Jack might just want to pick up the report and go, or he might want to go out for a drink to discuss it. Whatever happened, she would go with the flow, and she remembered to turn off her mobile phone, because if he stayed, she didn't want any interruptions.

There was a light knock at the door and, breathing deeply to try and steady herself, Jane answered. He looked so different, so disturbingly devastating. Dressed in black chinos, pale grey linen shirt and black cashmere sweater, his curly hair slightly tamed by gel. No leathers or crash helmet, but still the same twinkling blue eyes, the curving lips, the lean body. He held out a bottle of wine.

"Thanks," Jane said, taking the bottle from him and edging awkwardly back into the small room.

"Can I pour you one, or I've got lager if

you prefer?"

It all sounded a bit formal.

"Just a lager," he replied. "I'm driving. Are you okay here, or did you want to go out, I really don't mind?" he asked.

Jane had put two copies of the report on the coffee table. She poured the drinks and set them down beside the papers. She waved at the two-seater sofa.

"I'm fine here. Sit down. I'm afraid it's the only soft seat I have."

They sat, side by side, and Jane realised that the uneven springs and cushions on the tatty sofa were pushing them both towards the middle. She was aware of the warmth of his body, and the clean scent of his after-shave, as he leaned forward and picked up the printed report.

"This looks good," he smiled. "Might as well give it a read through now."

"I hope it's what your friend wants? Remember, the day was all new to me."

"That's fine, a totally fresh approach."

He took out a gold pen and picked up the report. To her surprise, he became very business-like, reading the pages thoroughly, stopping now and then to ask a further question: the temperature of the water in the pool, the number of staff on reception, was there enough privacy in the changing rooms?

She answered clearly, casting her mind back and re-living the day as the questions rolled on. He made notes on the back of the papers with his expensive looking pen, and Jane realised that this really was an in-depth survey of the Spa. Either he had a very meticulous friend who owned it, or maybe he had something to do with the running of it himself. Questions began to tumble around in her mind, questions she wanted to ask, but she held back, and every time he leaned forward to make a note, she was aware of his lean thigh rubbing against hers. His hand brushed hers as they both picked up their drinks. The tension was building within her and Jane was almost sure that he, too, was feeling the same. At last he had finished and put the report back on the table.

"That's a great job," he said.

"Thanks. I know I keep saying it, but it was a great birthday."

He relaxed, stretched his arm along the back of the sofa and playfully ran his fingers through her hair.

"And the haircut. It still looks good."

Jane was melting. She turned towards him, their eyes locked together and it seemed that there was nothing in the world except this small room and the unstable sofa. He held her gaze and brought his hands up to hold either side of her head, so that she was captured in his grasp.

"I want you Jane," he said softly. "You've knocked me off balance, but I'm not entirely free."

"I guessed that, but *I am*," Jane's voice caught.

"Are you sure this is what you want?" he asked.

She moved nearer and their lips met. It was right. It had to be. She had never experienced such a strong physical attraction. She knew hardly anything about him, but she was willing to take a chance, no questions, no thoughts about the future, this was here and now. She wanted him and felt the same response in him. They held tightly to each other as their kisses became more urgent. Jane untangled herself and stood, holding out her hands to him. He held her against him, their need arising. Quickly, they moved into the bedroom. In spite of herself and her arousal, Jane felt her usual self-consciousness about her body as she started to undress in the candlelit room and turned away.

"Don't hide, I want to see you," Jack said, turning her round and pulling her closer. "You're beautiful."

Jane was swept away. The evening drifted into night as they made love on the small bed, their bodies close and their needs overwhelming. Jane was lost, Jack was passionate and skilled, nothing like the hasty, beery efforts of Greg.

They lay together afterwards, exhausted, contented, wrapped in each other. There was no need for words or promises of love, they took the moment and lived for it.

§

It was just getting light when Jane awoke and turned sleepily, remembering the fabulous, unexpected night. She became aware that she was alone and sat up quickly, looking around. Surely he hadn't gone without waking her? The bedroom door opened and she clutched the sheet around her as Jack entered the room. He was dressed, his hair damp from the shower, and there was a faint scent of her exclusive shower gel. He came towards her and sat on the side of the bed. Gently, he reached over and pulled the sheet down, kissing her curvaceous breasts.

"I've got to go now. I'm flying to France later today, for a couple of weeks. I'll contact you when I'm back in London, if you want me to?"

"Yes, yes, I do," Jane replied, reaching up and put her arms round him.

"Jane, things are complicated. I can't make any promises at the moment, but when I come back we'll need to talk. Are you willing to trust me on this?"

"Yes, I'm at a bit of a crossroads myself, I can't think clearly about my future," she replied.

They kissed a lingering goodbye and Jane unlocked the door. As he left, she walked to the window and looked out onto the

deserted, early morning street. Jack was
getting into a large, black car, sleek and
expensive looking, with shaded windows. It
was yet another mystery about him - from
leather-clad   biker   to   passionate,
accomplished lover, to wealthy looking
businessman. She was aware that she knew
hardly anything about him. Where was this
all going to end? Jane shivered with
apprehension, but knew that wherever this
led her, she was not going to hold back. For
once in her life she was going all the way.

CHAPTER SEVEN

For the next week Jane tried to concentrate on sorting out her life. She wanted to change things. She had finished with Greg, which was a start, but there were more changes to make. Most of all she wanted to see Jack and talk, as he had promised. The thought filled her with a mixture of excitement and apprehension; she had no idea what he was going to reveal. There was a mystery about him which intrigued her, she had to try and stop herself longing for him.

In the meantime, she was determined to try to find another job. It was totally boring sitting in front of a screen all day, entering figures onto spread sheets. She wanted to be out in the real world, face to face with people. She knew that her lack of qualifications would make it difficult to find anything challenging, but decided to spend her lunch hours visiting employment agencies. She felt she had more chance of getting something better if she appeared in person, rather than on the internet.

However, the signs were not good. It all seemed a bit useless. Qualifications were the answer for the more interesting jobs, otherwise it was just more office and computer work. She found that she was getting back to the office later and later, as she spread her search wider during her lunch breaks.

At the end of the week, she flopped down in a little organic, whole-food cafe. She was hungry and tired and a little shaky. She needed a drink and food before she went back to work. Over a cup of green tea and chicken salad sandwich, she looked around. The cafe was small, and brightly decorated, the wooden furniture didn't match and the tables and chairs were painted in all the colours of the rainbow. On each table stood a jam jar filled with fresh flowers. From the back, in the kitchen, she heard the sound of someone singing. The atmosphere was busy and happy and she was reluctant to tear herself away and go back to her desk and the sterile office. She looked at her watch and was concerned to see that she was running out of time. She stood to leave, and saw a printed notice on the counter - *temporary part-time help required* – and on an impulse, she turned and spoke to the young woman behind the till.

"Do you know how many hours?" she asked, nodding towards the notice.

The woman came towards her. She was small, dark and faintly hippie looking, with a long cotton dress and her unruly hair tied back with a floaty scarf.

"It's just four days, Monday to Thursday. Are you interested?" she asked.

"Yes." Jane felt she would like to work in this lively little cafe.

"We're a family business. My husband Luigi, who is in the kitchen, makes all the bread and cakes, and my mother-in-law usually helps out, but she's had an operation and will be off for a few months. We have a couple of students who come in at the weekend, so it's just the weekdays."

She came around the counter and waved to an empty table. Jane sat down and the young woman sat opposite her.

"I'm Maria," she said. "I do all the other work at the moment, so we need someone who doesn't mind generally helping out, it could be taking the money, serving tables, washing up. Do you have any experience?"

Jane explained that at the moment she was working in an office on computer data, and saw that Maria looked doubtful.

"It would be very different and probably less money," she said.

At that moment Luigi broke into song from the kitchen and Maria laughed. "That's another problem," she said.

Suddenly, Jane wanted to be part of this relaxed group. Even if it was only temporary and paid less money, it would give her a breathing space, time to think about her future.

"I worked on a cruise ship a few years ago," she said. "It was very flexible, we had to help out with anything that needed doing, and look after all sorts of needs for the passengers. I think I could do the job."

Maria nodded. "That's good experience. Perhaps we could try it out?"

Jane eagerly agreed, she would start the following Monday and they would see how it went.

§

She walked back to the office in a dream. She knew that she would have to completely reorganise her own expenses, cut back a lot; four days work a week on a lower wage would simply not be enough to live on. Perhaps she could find a Friday or weekend job to supplement the money. She drifted back to the office, her head full of plans, anything to make a change in her life.

"Nice of you to remember where you work!"

Steve, the Office Manager, was standing next to her desk when she hurried in.

"Can you come into my office please?"

Jane knew that she had been late several times recently and was not really concentrating on her work, but as she followed him into the small office, she became annoyed at his pompous manner. They had never really got on as she refused to pander to him. He sat down and motioned her to the chair opposite. He leaned back, assessing her, dragging out the moment, trying to make her feel uneasy. She realised that she really disliked him. He expected people to massage his ego and she had never tried. Sometimes he'd made subtle, hidden comments about her size, nothing she could really challenge him with, but uncomfortable and hurtful all the same.

"You haven't been keeping up with the work lately," he said, "and also this isn't the first time you've taken extra lunchtime without permission."

He was watching her carefully, obviously enjoying the moment.

"It's a hard world out there, you know," he continued, "and you're lucky to have this job. I need to tell you that unless you make an effort to increase your work rate and get here on time, otherwise I'll have to issue you with an official written warning."

Jane could see that he had been building himself up to this moment of power. He expected her to crumble, beg to be given a chance to improve, to work extra hours, anything to save her job.

"Actually, don't bother," she said, feeling herself growing in confidence, picturing the busy little cafe.

"I'm leaving anyway. In fact, if you don't mind I think I'll just collect my things and go now. You can post me any paperwork. Nice speaking to you, Steve."

With a wild feeling of release, Jane stalked out of the office, back to her desk and collected her belongings. She could see the other staff watching in amazement in the open-plan office.

"Goodbye everyone," she called. "I'm off, and if you fancy nice lunch-time snacks, visit the Garden Cafe a few streets away, I can recommend it!"

She was free. She had taken the first step in her new life, now she would just have to work out how to afford it.

§

That evening Jane rang her mother. They usually caught up with a long phone call each week, and she told her all about the job situation.

At first, her mother was appalled.

"You've given up a safe office job to work in a café, and it's only *temporary*?" she asked.

"I have a feeling it could be more," Jane replied. "They seem to be very busy and the atmosphere's great. I think the business is growing. Anyway, I just needed a change."

"And how about money?"

It was back to the old problem, and Jane confessed that she would have to look for some extra hours work at the weekends. There was a silence, then her mother spoke, a little hesitantly.

"What about Victoria?" she said.

"How do you mean?" Jane asked.

"Well, you know how she's struggling until she has the baby, trying to work full-time. They have plenty of money. Why not ask if she would like some cleaning, shopping or general help on a Friday, so she can rest at the weekends? I'm sure she'd leap at it."

Jane wasn't certain how to respond. It was perfectly true that Victoria could do with some help, they had the money to pay for it and the minimal house should be easy to clean. But how would she feel about her twin being her employer, and what about Julian's reaction? As the questions tumbled around in her mind, her mother seemed to sense what she was thinking.

"The house would be empty on Fridays while they're at work. You could have a key and come and go when you wanted. I know it might feel awkward at first, but you'd be helping Victoria out."

There was a pause while Jane thought about the idea.

"Do you want me to suggest it?" her mother asked.

"Well ... okay then. But if she's interested, tell her to ring me. Don't commit me to anything until I've spoken to her."

It was a possible solution to the problem, but Jane wondered if it was the right one. She would have to wait and see how Victoria felt.

§

Jane had a few days to herself before she started her new job. It would be very different, being on her feet all day, dealing with people, instead of sitting down in front of a screen. For a fleeting moment, she wondered if being physically busy instead of sitting down at work might help her lose a few pounds. Then she remembered what Jack had said about not bothering with diets, he liked her as she was, and that was a new idea to get used to. She had felt comfortable with Maria, the owner, and wanted to meet the tuneful Luigi. She decided that she would have to sort out her clothes - she wouldn't need the smart office gear anymore and needed to see what she had in her wardrobe which would be suitable for her new lifestyle.

She wished that she could talk to Jack, but he'd said he would be in France for a while and so she resisted the temptation to try and contact him. It would be great if she could have another weekend at the Spa, get herself relaxed and toned again, but that was just a day-dream. It was good to be free from the office and the overbearing Steve, she smiled when she recalled his face as she walked out. So many changes suddenly in her life, so many new things to adjust to.

To Jane's surprise, Victoria rang and begged her to help out on Fridays. She would be so happy if Jane could just go round the house and tidy up, so that everything was neat and ready for the weekend. She would leave a note and money if any shopping was needed. They would pay her generously in cash and Victoria said she would bring a take-away meal home each Friday night so they could eat together. Victoria actually seemed pleased with the idea.

Friday was Julian's night out with the guys from work! Jane accepted, they had a deal, one part of her plan was in place, she would concentrate on putting a lot of effort into the new arrangements. It would give her something to keep her busy. She wanted the time to pass quickly so that Jack Flynn would be back from France and, perhaps, ready to talk. He was still a bit of a stranger to her and she hoped that he was serious about seeing her again. She was tempted to tell Victoria about him, she really needed someone to confide in. She felt that she was bursting to talk about him. However, she knew what her twin's reaction would be.

Sleeping with a man she hardly knew, waiting around for him to sort out his complicated life, which she knew nothing about. No, it would be unthinkable to the organised Victoria.

Jane realised that it was best to say nothing, keep her secret for the moment and hope that she was not mistaken in trusting the captivating Irishman.

CHAPTER EIGHT

The week passed quickly as Jane began to learn the work at the cafe. Maria was a whirlwind: taking orders, serving food and drinks, clearing tables, and chatting to the customers. She showed Jane the routine, then left her to get on with it, unless she needed help. Jane threw herself into the new experience. The cafe was buzzing, the food good and the staff great to work with. She spent a lot of time clearing and washing up, and helping tidy up after Luigi in the kitchen. There was a real family atmosphere and they knew most of their customers. Jane worked hard and flopped down pleasantly exhausted when she got back home in the evenings. She was surprised to find that she fell into a deep sleep the moment her head hit the pillow, and awoke refreshed the next day. The work was physical but not stressful and she began to enjoy it.

To her delight she received a short text from Jack to say he was busy sorting out some urgent business, but hoped to be back in London soon. No date was mentioned, and she knew that this was how it was going to be. She found that instead of being on edge about this, she was oddly excited by the unpredictability of his casual arrangements.

By the time Friday came, she was ready to tackle Victoria's house. Julian picked her up early and gave her a lift to Wimbledon. He passed her bunch of keys and a full page of notes from Victoria.

"Help yourself to drinks and food," he said. "There's plenty in the fridge." He hesitated. "If it goes okay and you want to do it next week, I'll pick you up again."

"It's just a temporary arrangement, Julian, until Victoria feels better."

"I know. When the baby comes we'll get

proper help."

Jane found it difficult to decide whether he resented her helping Victoria, or whether he was just making sure she wasn't expecting it to be permanent. Go to work and earn your big money, Julian, she wanted to say, and let Victoria and me sort it out between us.

It was strange letting herself into the expansive house and it felt completely different being there on her own. She wandered around, taking in the generous size of the downstairs rooms, square hall, large lounge, separate dining room, office, snug TV room and enormous state of the art kitchen and utility room, shower and toilet, plus a spacious, sunny conservatory. To her surprise, although all the furniture and fittings were new and of the highest quality, the whole area appeared a little neglected, dusty, and untidy. Jane went up the wide stairs and began to take stock, very aware of the fact that she had never been in any of these other rooms apart from the guest bathroom.

There were five bedrooms, all of them en-suite. The largest was obviously Victoria and Julian's room and Jane was amazed at the untidy clutter. It looked as though they had both been late for work: clothes and shoes flung about, books, newspapers and magazines on the floor, make up bottles and jars, brushes and hair products strewn across the whole of the fitted dressing table. There was a huge en-suite bathroom with double sinks, free standing bath and a large power shower, beautifully equipped with the latest designer equipment. Soggy towels littered the floor and, if she was honest, the room was a little grubby. It needed a complete proper clean.

Between the bedroom and bathroom there were two walk-in wardrobes – his and hers. Jane slid open the doors to gaze in wonder at Victoria's rows of designer clothes. Suits in black, navy and grey, blouses in dazzling white and blue, casual trousers, jumpers, tops, evening and classic wear, and rows of shoes. All arranged neatly, rows and rows of them. At least Victoria had managed to look after her clothes before she wore them, afterwards discarding them around the bedroom. Peering in, Jane was surprised to discover a row of new maternity outfits, all subdued colours, expensive looking, and she was only four months pregnant! It was difficult to reconcile the orderly wardrobe and the forward planning for the baby with the untidy bedroom and the dusty, slightly neglected house.

Jane was tempted to peek into Julian's cupboards, no doubt he also had loads of designer suits for business and trendy casual gear. She wondered whether he also had a secret hoard of special magazines and DVDs stowed away. Hurriedly, she pushed the thought from her mind and slid the door closed, then went and sat down on the huge unmade bed.

It was going to be impossible to restore order and give the whole place a clean in just one day. She texted Victoria and suggested that she would just concentrate on the downstairs and save the upstairs for next week. To her relief, Victoria agreed.

The day passed quickly as Jane tackled the enormous downstairs space, stopping only for a quick snack and coffee. Before she'd finished, she realised that Victoria would soon be back. She felt exhausted and dishevelled. If it was going to be a regular arrangement, she would bring a change of clothes in future and ask if she could shower in one of the spare bathrooms at the end of the day.

Victoria was home early, clutching Chinese take away. "I know what you like," she said.

She looked around with pleasure and exclaimed at the tidy, transformed downstairs and went to get a glass of wine for Jane. They settled at the kitchen table and Victoria handed Jane an envelope of money.

"Let's get that out of the way, so we can relax," she said. "Oh, and we decided we must pay for you to have a taxi home."

It was okay; it seemed that they could make the arrangement work. Jane had been worried that she might feel awkward taking money from her twin, but she had certainly earned it and decided that in future she would pace herself better, not wear herself out so much.

"So, how's the sickness, dare I ask?" she said, looking at Victoria, who was a little pale.

"Getting a bit better. I can eat at night

now, but I still feel terrible in the mornings."

Jane sympathised. That would explain the chaos in the house: it must be difficult for Victoria to cope with sickness when she was rushing to get ready for work. Jane thought that her efforts would certainly help for a few weeks.

"And how about you?" Victoria asked, picking at her chow mein. "Still not seeing Greg?"

"Oh no. That's definitely over," Jane replied. "I'm just concentrating on my new job at the moment."

A wave of emotions suddenly struck her. She wanted to confide in Victoria about Jack. In the past they'd always shared information about boyfriends, but she held back. Jack wasn't a boy and he wasn't around. How could she explain that to her twin?

Jane was beginning to wilt. The exhausting day, the food and wine were taking their toll. She thought she would ask Victoria to call a taxi, when just then her own mobile rang. She scrabbled in her bag, quickly answering, hoping it wasn't that wretched Greg.

"Where are you? I'm at your place, I want to see you."

It was Jack! Her heart began to race and her hands were trembling with unexpected anticipation.

"I'm at my sister's house," she said.

"Can you get away? I could pick you up." His voice was urgent.

"Ok, I'll be ready," she said, giving him the address and then switched off to see Victoria staring at her in surprise, reading her body language.

"It's someone I know," Jane explained, "just back from France. Forget the taxi, he's going to pick me up."

Suddenly she was aware of her untidy appearance – old jeans and top, trainers and unruly hair. She took a deep breath. She must ask a favour and hope her twin would agree.

"Victoria, sorry to ask, but if I could have a quick wash upstairs, do you have a top you could lend me that would fit? And can I have a hairbrush and use a squirt of some of your perfume?" It all came tumbling out as Victoria watched her with a smile.

"How long have you got? Is this guy someone special?" she asked.

"Not long enough," Jane replied, on edge. "Can we fix it? I'll tell you more another time."

§

There was a firm knock on the door, and Jane answered, with Victoria hovering in the hall behind her, trying to get a good look.

Jack stood there, exactly as he had been at the Spa: black leathers, crash helmet in hand, the huge bike looming behind him on the driveway. Quickly she introduced him to Victoria, smiling inside at the astonished look on her twin's face. He was certainly not what she had expected. Jane took the spare helmet that he passed to her. She was aware that her sister was dumbstruck by the sudden and unexpected end to their evening.

She could sense the tension in the air, the magnetism between them as he fastened the straps under Jane's chin, kissing the end of her nose. She had no idea where he was going to take her – back to her flat, a hotel, or did he have somewhere else arranged?

Jane didn't know, and as she mounted the pillion seat and waved goodbye to the bemused Victoria, she didn't care. Wherever Jack took her would be fine. It may not be the most sensible way to act, but when she was totally in his hands, sense seemed to fly out of the window.

CHAPTER NINE

It was an apartment: a penthouse, a spacious, super-cool living space overlooking the river Thames. Jane looked out of the plate glass windows, down onto the river, and across to the Houses of Parliament, the whole of the Embankment and the London city skyline lit up before her eyes. She turned to Jack.

"Is this your place? I had no idea."

Jack was peeling off his jacket. He nodded and gathered her in his arms, holding and kissing her urgently.

"We can talk later," he murmured into her hair. "I want you now."

Effortlessly he picked her up and carried her into the bedroom – a huge, high bed, dark wooden floors, the walls painted in a deep, rich, chalky red, subdued lighting. She was aware of glimpses of the room as they fell onto the bed. At last, they were together, and her need was almost desperate after their time apart. Being with Jack was all she wanted. There was no feeling of self-consciousness about her body this time. He wanted her as she was, all of her, and she gave herself to him willingly.

§

They lay back, tangled together, exhausted but content.

"This is the time I should light us both a cigarette," Jack said, raising himself onto one elbow and gazing down at her. "But I don't think you smoke."

"Gave it up when I was twenty-one," she replied.

"Joint?" he asked quietly.

"Really?" she was intrigued. How many things she had to learn about him.

"Not if you don't want to. Champagne?

There must be something I can tempt you with."

Jane smiled to herself as he went to get the bottle and glasses. There certainly *was* something he could tempt her with anytime, she thought, as she watched his fit, naked body walk from the room. It was a dream, a fantasy, the sort of thing that happened to other people. What could he possibly see in plump Jane Harkness?

Jack returned to bed and passed her a glass of chilled, sparkling champagne.

"Now," he said, "bring me up to date. I want to know about your job, and your ex-. Has he been in touch? Do I need to warn him off? And what you were doing at your sister's house?"

Jane sipped her drink and slowly told Jack everything: about finding work at the Garden Cafe, walking out on Steve and the boring job, and helping out Victoria for the extra money. He listened carefully.

"So, you're living in that little flat, struggling for money and cleaning for your twin?" he asked quietly.

"It's okay, I'll manage. I just feel happier. It's only a temporary arrangement anyway."

Jane really wanted to have a shower. She had been slaving away at housework all day and then had been swept straight to bed with Jack. He led her to a large wet room, turned on the power shower and grabbed the gel. Jane squealed with delight as they played under the water, all her old inhibitions blown away, soaping each other, kissing and exploring. Suddenly, he gripped her shoulders, pushing her back against the wet tiles. He was urgent, demanding, and Jane had never felt so desired in her life.

Afterwards, he wrapped her in an enormous white towel and found her one of his robes, then led the way into the living room. The lights were dimmed, a leather couch stood before the windows with their fantastic view of London by night, a coffee table with a bottle of red wine and two crystal glasses stood ready.

They slid down into the deep, soft leather seats and Jack handed her a glass. Just then, she heard the chimes of Big Ben, filling the room.

"It's midnight!" she exclaimed. "Where did the time go?"

"The witching hour," Jack said, "but

you're not going anywhere just yet, Cinderella. It's time I told you everything."

Jane felt her stomach flip and her breath catch. She had wanted to know all about Jack, but suddenly the thought filled her with apprehension. In spite of their fantastic love making, he was still a bit of a stranger to her. She'd been astonished at his apartment and obvious wealth, but what else was he going to reveal?

"I want to tell it to you from the start, so you'll understand," he began, slipping his arm around her shoulders, pulling her close, and settling back into the sofa.

"I come from the far west of Ireland. My father worked at a racehorse training stable, and we lived in a cottage in the grounds. He was born with some sort of natural affinity with horses. They trusted him and he got the best out of them. That's where I grew up: out in the sticks with horses and my little sister for company."

He paused for a moment, then continued.

"He could have been a trainer himself, but he was so unreliable. When he was at the races, if he won, the money always went

back on the next race, and at the end of the
day, he would finish off spending all his
winnings at the pub. It was such a waste.
Eventually, my mother left him and took
my sister to live with relatives in Dublin. I
was sixteen at the time, and the owner of
the stables found me a job, so I stayed.
When my father was sober, I learned
everything there was to know about
breeding and training horses, and I was
hooked. Then, one night, he staggered out
of the pub in the dark, blind drunk, straight
under the wheels of a lorry."

At this, Jack picked up his glass and took
a slow drink, and Jane waited quietly for the
rest of the story, intrigued and unwilling to
break the spell.

"When that happened, I was twenty, I left
Ireland and decided to see something of the
world. With nothing in my pockets, I
hitched my way around Europe for a couple
of years. I enjoyed being free, and got casual
work on the way, living in hostels. I finally
made my way to France and found a job at
a vineyard in Bordeaux. It was great, the
sun was shining, there were French girls
around, so I stayed. I got myself an old

bicycle and explored the countryside in my time off. One day, I was cycling down a narrow lane when I saw a woman on a horse in front of me. The horse was magnificent, but too big and too strong for her. She was struggling and losing control, it was dangerous. I threw my bike in the ditch and caught them up. I managed to get hold of the bridle and stop him, then I told her to get off. I calmed the horse down, and said we should lead him home. That's how I met Claudine."

Claudine? Jane wanted to ask who she was, and where this was going, but managed to resist.

"When she showed me where she lived, I was staggered. A beautiful chateau, set in an estate, and the stables were out of this world. She had two ponies that she'd kept from her childhood and three more fantastic thoroughbred horses. They were well fed and groomed, but they needed exercise and proper training. It turned out that she only used the chateau at the weekends and had a young lad looking after the horses, who didn't know much about them. She offered me a job and a flat over the stables. It was just a dream chance for me, so I took it and moved in. I taught Claudine how to ride properly, too. She really had no idea."

Jack paused again, and for some time he was silent. He seemed to be carefully considering how to continue with the next part of his story.

"Claudine was thirty-three," he said eventually. "She'd inherited the chateau from her father, and taken over a successful beauty business from her mother. She had an apartment in Paris where the head office was based. She was very elegant, sophisticated, very French and chic, and also very rich. When she came back to the countryside at the weekends, she just wanted to drop the world of work and relax. We began riding together, eating together and, of course, eventually sleeping together."

Jack stopped and again picked up his glass. He turned towards Jane, looking deep into her eyes.

"I'm being honest here, keeping nothing back. We loved each other. She was dazzling to me with her lifestyle and wealth, and I think I appealed to her because I was young and because of my carefree ways. Also, the sex was pretty good."

Jane found it difficult to hear. She tried to picture the young, footloose Jack and the older, experienced Frenchwoman. She stayed silent. The many questions fizzing around in her mind might get answered tonight.

"We had a great year, and then, to our surprise, Claudine found she was pregnant. It was the last thing in the world she had planned, but I didn't want any child of mine to be born outside marriage. It was the old Irish Catholic upbringing kicking in. So, we got married and had Amelie. She's ten now. We never regretted that decision. We began to expand the business, turning exclusive hotels into beauty spas, increasing the cosmetic products side. At the same, I persuaded her to also invest in the horses, I now breed and race several top winners. As far as business is concerned, we gel. We're partners and very wealthy. As far as our marriage goes, we're still friends, but a couple of years ago we agreed on an open marriage. The love had faded. Claudine has her apartment in Paris and I keep this place in London. I come over for the races and horse sales here and in Ireland. We've both had affairs, but we've been discreet and always kept things civilised between us for Amelie's sake. There have been a lot of girls over the past two years, young, beautiful ..."

Jane wasn't sure she wanted to hear this.

"Don't turn away," he said, his voice commanding. "But they have mostly been immature, shallow, attracted by the money."

It was a lot to take in. Married, with a daughter that he obviously adored, wealthy, free to indulge in discreet relationships. Jane felt that perhaps she was learning more than she had wanted to know. Where did *she* fit into all this?

"Then, back in London, just out giving the bike a ride, I met you. It felt very different, and when I collected you from the Spa, you looked so happy and lovely. You got on the bike with no fuss, and we had fun at the chip shop. It was all so normal. Your didn't know anything about me – my wealth, my background, but you went with me anyway, just took me as I was. I knew then that what I had wanted for some time was a simpler life. No more travelling the world on business. A place in the country, more children, dogs, horses and a wife in the kitchen making me Irish stew." As he said it, his eyes were shining, teasing her again.

"I've never made Irish stew in my life," Jane replied. A wife, he'd said. Could he be serious?

"But you can learn," he replied, holding her. "I know it's happened quickly, but I want to be with you and I sense you feel the same."

Jane nodded, overwhelmed, unable to even speak.

"It will take time to arrange with the French lawyers. There'll be the divorce and custody arrangements, also the businesses will have to be untangled. That will be complex. The beauty side of things has always been Claudine's, but I travelled a lot and helped expand it. Over the years, I've found the places to buy, overseen the renovations. The horse breeding is worth millions, but I persuaded Claudine to invest back in the first place. Without her money it couldn't have got off the ground. When I arrived at the chateau I had nothing but a rucksack and a head full of knowledge about horses. Claudine invested in me. With the two businesses, we're practically billionaires."

Jane gasped, unable to take it all in. "I had no idea," she murmured.

"That's what I like, you just thought I was a guy with a motor bike and took a chance on me."

There was a sliver of pale, yellow light in the sky over the river, on the horizon.

"It's getting light, we've talked all night," Jane said. Her mind was in a whirl. He had said he would get a divorce, and that he wanted her in his life, but what about love? Was it too soon? They hardly knew each other.

"You said you're struggling to pay the rent," Jack said, ruffling her hair, and kissing her neck. "Stay here. It's the answer. I'm away quite a lot and it's empty, so you could move in. Or I could buy you a house, anywhere you want."

It was all happening so quickly .The ground was shaking beneath her feet. Jane tried to imagine herself living in this fantastic apartment.

"I've got the new job to think about," she replied unsteadily.

"Of course. Carry on with it, help your sister, do what you want, but be here for me, Jane. I want to think of you living here when I'm away and I want you here in my bed when I come back."

He was so open in his demands. Jane felt utterly overwhelmed.

"It makes me sound like your mistress," she answered quietly. "I don't want you to shower me with presents or give me money."

"A casual mistress, but just a temporary one. Or a lover. You'll have to take me on trust. It may take time, and it will mean I'm in France most of the time, but I'll sort things out. Now, it's Saturday. You have a day to make up your mind. It's your decision. Tomorrow, if you want to go along with the idea, we could move you in here."

AN IRISH PASSION

PART TWO

CHAPTER TEN

"You're really living *here*?"

Victoria twirled around the huge living room, taking in the space, the expensive furniture, the views over the river and the city.

Jane had invited her twin to visit the penthouse. It was time to tell her all about Jack.

"Yes, it's fabulous," Jane replied. "There are guest rooms, a roof garden, home cinema, games room, everything you could imagine."

"And this belongs to the guy on the motorbike?" Victoria was full of questions, completely staggered and openly impressed at Jane's new surroundings.

Jane put two cups of coffee down on the table. "I'll tell you all about him."

It was a relief to finally confide in someone, and, at the end of the day, Victoria was the only person she could talk to openly. Since Victoria's difficult pregnancy and Jane's new found romance, the scales seemed to have tipped the other way. Jane no longer felt envy for her twin's lifestyle. She was happy herself, fulfilled. She knew it was because of her feelings for Jack; with or without the money she was head over heels in love with him, and more confident in herself. She spilled out the whole story, from their first meeting, through their brief times together, to moving in with him. He had gone back to France to start making arrangements for the future and Jane was living in his apartment on her own.

Victoria sat spellbound, listening intently. She took it all in quietly, no questions during the story, and waited until Jane had finished.

"Well? What do you think?" Jane wanted

her honest opinion.

"I can see the attraction between you," Victoria began. "It was obvious to me even when he picked you up. This is just a dream location, but what about the future, Jane? You joked about being his casual mistress, but what if that's really all he wants?"

"I've thought it through and I trust him. I know what you're thinking: why me? I've gone over that myself, several times. I'm not slim, pretty, or elegantly dressed, but he seems to want me as I am. Just for once, a man who doesn't try to change me. And I'm madly in love, I can't help it."

"I'm not trying to talk you out of anything, but you *have* made some mistakes in the past. Don't be carried away by the fantastic sex, or dazzled by his money," Victoria warned.

Jane knew that this time her sister wasn't putting her down, just trying to be cautious.

"I didn't know anything about his wealth at first. I'm not giving up my job and I'll still help you out, so I'll have my own money to spend. He hasn't showered me with presents or gifts, and I've said I don't want him to. We just have fun together, and the sex is amazing. I'm grabbing this chance. To be honest, I think I would even accept being his mistress, if that's the only way to be together."

"Well, in that case, go for it!" Victoria replied.

§

In the weeks that followed, Jane's life was busy and exciting. She worked at the cafe, helped Victoria one day a week, and some weekends, when he could arrange it, Jack would fly back from France. The apartment was so different when he arrived. Noisy, untidy, bursting with energy. Jack filled the space and would turn her world upside-down. Sometimes they spent the time alone, sending out for food, lying in bed, catching up, unable to get enough of each other. At other times he was restless, wanting to explore London, eat out, visit a pub with live music. They rode into the countryside on the huge, black bike, occasionally staying overnight at a little country inn he knew deep in the Cotswolds countryside. In the honey-coloured stone hideaway next to the village green, they ate, drank and then slept in a four-poster bed.

"I feel as though we're in another age," Jane murmured happily. "You could be a knight riding out to take some secret information to the king."

"And who are you?" he queried.

"Oh just the wench from the bar that you've seduced."

"You're just getting carried away," he smiled.

"Is the Chateau like this, full of history?"

There was a silence; they very rarely talked about Jack's life in France, unless he raised the subject.

"It's very large and beautiful. Set in landscaped gardens and the countryside around is mostly vineyards. The furniture is all French antique, some of it quite heavy, but Claudine has a knack of making things seem softer – floaty curtains, fancy bed linen and so on."

"And do you sleep with her?" It had slipped out, the question that she had longed to ask every time he returned to France.

"Where are you going with this, Jane?" he

said, sitting up, moving slightly away from her and leaning back against the pillows.

"I just need to know, even if it hurts."

"Not since I met you," he replied. "Before that, then the answer is sometimes. I told you we've both had affairs in the last couple of years. Mostly I was seeing young girls who just wanted to spend my money and Claudine was seeing an older lawyer in Paris. If we were at the Chateau at the weekends with Amelie, perhaps in the summer when we had all been out riding, swimming in the pool and eating and drinking, then, yes, we did end the day in bed together. But, as I just told you, not since I met you. Can you accept that?"

"Yes, I don't know why I get so unsure of myself, it just that I feel I hadn't lived until I met you," Jane murmured, holding him close. "You're all I want."

"That's lucky, because you have me."

He slipped his arms round her, pulling her down, under the covers, into the high, soft bed.

§

Jack was unpredictable, funny, and full of life. When he went away, life was different. The penthouse seemed too quiet, too tidy and organised and Jane missed him with an ache she had never experienced before.

He told her that he and Claudine were officially separated; the divorce would be arranged and the business interests would be divided in a fair way. Most of all, he stressed that Amelie must be considered. After all, the chateau would be hers to inherit eventually and he wanted to cause her as little distress as possible.

"She lives in Paris with Claudine and goes to school there," he told Jane. "They usually go back to the chateau at weekends and in the school holidays."

Jane knew that she would never be part of that scenario. Her life with Jack would be separate, but perhaps she could meet the little French girl sometime, get to know her when things were settled. It was difficult to imagine what Jack's daughter might be like.

§

As Autumn passed and Winter approached,

Victoria grew bigger. The pregnancy was still exhausting her and Jane helped when she could. She felt a little concerned. She wished that she felt she could talk to Julian, find out if he was attending any sort of ante-natal classes with Victoria, getting advice and being considerate, but found him rather remote.

She talked to her mother about her concerns, and Marion agreed to keep an eye on things. It didn't seem so long ago that Victoria had been the one with the perfect life, but Jane no longer envied her.

She had Jack – not all the time and never consistently; he would come, disrupt her days and fill her nights, then go just as quickly, leaving her exhausted. But still, she wouldn't change things for the world.

At the beginning of December, he rang her from France.

"Is your passport up to date?" he asked.

"Yes, why?" Jane was thrilled, wondering what he had planned.

"The weekend after this, get some time off, I'm taking you to New York."

"Wow, New York! You mean it?"

"Of course. Don't most girls like to do

some Christmas shopping there?" he asked. "But have you been before?"

"Never, I've always wanted to go."

A whole long weekend with Jack, in New York? Life just got better and better ...

§

Jack had made all the arrangements: club class flight, a suite at the Park Lane Hotel overlooking Central Park, leaflets for her to browse and decide what to see.

"Let's do some of the real tourist sights," Jane said, excitedly. "Empire State Building, Central Park, Times Square, I want to see them all."

"That's fine," he answered, "but we'll go to some of the big stores on the last day."

New York was all Jane had ever expected and more – big, pushy, throbbing with life, exhausting, but most of all exhilarating. Being with Jack was a bonus. He had visited many times before and was a perfect guide. He found places to eat and Irish bars where he tried to introduce her to Guinness. After sight-seeing, they made their way back to the hotel in the early evenings and flopped into bed. She had him to herself, every delicious inch of him, every night. She never wanted the break to end. As they explored the city together, they talked. Sitting in a small, intimate bar, Jack told her more about his life as a child in Ireland, how he missed his mother when she left, taking his little sister with her.

"I was left with my feckless father, out in the wilds, always broke," he explained. "Who would have thought that some years later I would be here in New York, able to afford whatever I want?"

They were getting to know each other more deeply. Jack told her about his previous relationships

"I had a great time when I was travelling around. Loads of girls, I have to admit, but we all grow up." He was cradling his glass, watching her reactions. "What about you, Jane, was there anyone special for you?" he asked.

Jane thought back, to her awkward teenage years, and her mindless quest for fun at uni, before she dropped out, her awareness of always being the less successful, plain twin, existing in Victoria's shadow.

"Not really," she sighed. "There were just a few casual boyfriends. I didn't have the confidence to think that someone would actually want to stay with me."

"Well, now you do," he smiled. "I've seen you change, even in the last few days."

Jane blossomed under his attention. She had bought a few new clothes before they flew out, more stylish and adventurous than her usual choice, and she enjoyed his compliments whenever she wore them. He didn't care what she ate or drank, either – no nagging to exercise or change her shape. Her confidence began to build. She was a woman in love and he really *wanted* her, just as she was.

The city was festooned in the most dazzling Christmas decorations, shop windows out-doing each other with their displays and lights. Jane felt that she had been transported to some magical Winter wonderland. She wished their time together could go on and on.

§

On the last day Jack hailed a cab as they left the hotel.

"I'm taking you to hit the stores and then Tiffany's," he said, and sure enough, they filled the day making last minute purchases, eating out and finishing at the expensive shop.

Breath-taking jewels, necklaces, bracelets, rings, watches, all laid out in style. Jane began to get the feeling that he was going to buy her a gift. He hesitated, slowly walking past the glossy counters. Past the rings – surely not, it was too early to think about *that*. Then he stopped near a range of beautiful watches.

"Have a look," he said. "What do you like?"

In a dream, Jane gazed at the rows. There was one she fancied, in an antique style. Small, round, with a pretty enamel face, surrounded by some sparkling stones, possibly diamonds and little seed pearls. She looked away, suddenly uneasy. This place was so expensive.

"That one?" he said gently. He had seen her interest and signalled to the assistant, who lifted the delicate watch onto the

AN IRISH PASSION
133

counter.

"That's a very good choice," the assistant smiled attentively back. "Platinum surrounded by diamonds, one of our best."

"Try it on," Jack said, turning to her as she fastened the exquisite piece of jewellery around her wrist.

"Do you like it?" he asked.

The assistant was smiling encouragingly, she could sense a sale.

"Yes," Jane replied. "But how much is it? it must be expensive."

"If you ask the cost, you'll get nothing," Jack snapped. Jane felt shaken, it was so sudden and unlike him. The assistant moved slightly away, politely giving them space and time to decide.

"Wrap it up, I'll take it," he growled, taking out his wallet and slamming his credit card onto the counter.

They were quiet on the way back to the hotel. It was their first disagreement and Jane wasn't quite sure how or why it had happened; so quickly and so out of the blue. He had obviously wanted to buy her a present, something to remember their time in New York and she had queried the cost.

It must be a sensitive area for him, but even so, Jane didn't like being put down in that way.

Back in their hotel room, Jack took off his warm overcoat and threw it on the bed. Taking the gift-wrapped parcel from the pocket of his coat, he placed it on the coffee table then went to the drinks cabinet and poured himself a large whisky.

Jane stood in front of him, her clenched hands in her pockets, a well of anger beginning to rise.

"I've told you I don't want expensive gifts. It's enough that I live in your apartment, be brought away with you, and I love it. But don't *buy me*, Jack, that's not what I want, not how it should be."

For a moment, his eyes blazed with anger, and she felt that maybe she had gone too far, but it had to be said.

Jane turned her back and crossed the room, putting distance between them, trying to calm down.

She stood at the window, looking down on the expanse of Central Park. It was their last night in New York together; she had wanted it to be perfect and it had all gone

AN IRISH PASSION   135

wrong. She realised that Jack was not an easy person. He was devastatingly handsome, fun, exciting, loving and generous, but at the same time she now knew that he was also volatile, mercurial, and used to getting his own way. The silence in the room was chilling.

"Oh, Jane, come here," he said.

She turned to see that he was holding his arms out to her.

"Don't be upset, I know I can be a bit quick tempered."

Jane felt some of the tension seeping from her body. She moved across the room into his arms, and they sank down onto the comfortable sofa.

"I wanted to buy you something, but it's a Christmas present. Save it until then, have something to open on Christmas Day, because I won't be with you."

"I hadn't thought about my Christmas plans yet," she replied. "This break has just taken it out of my mind."

"I was going to tell you. I'll be in France at the chateau. Claudine and I have decided to spend a family Christmas there, a last one for Amelie's sake. After that, we'll tell her about the future."

Jane knew that it was the decent thing to do, but she still felt distressed. They would be a family unit and she would be outside the circle. This was the sort of thing that happened to mistresses: she had read all about it in magazines, left alone at Christmas, New Year or holiday time. Was that really going to be her future?

It wouldn't be easy, but if she wanted Jack, for the time being, she supposed it would be part of the package.

"Think about what you'd like to do over Christmas," he said gently. "Invite anyone you want to stay at the apartment, order caterers, go somewhere extravagant, abroad if you like, take the family, whatever you fancy. Perhaps you'll even let me pay for it."

He was obviously trying to lighten the atmosphere.

"Oh, I'll just go to my parents, it'll be fine," she said.

He held her in his arms, stroking her, nuzzling her, and she could smell the faint trace of whisky on his breath.

"I know it's hard for you, but it's difficult for me too," he said. "I'm breaking up a big part of my life. You have to trust me Jane, I'll sort out the future."

"I'll try." It was all Jane could answer at that moment.

"It's our last night here, what are we doing, wasting time arguing. Come to bed, be good and say thank you for your present."

There was amusement in his voice, and she knew he was teasing her, testing her reaction, arousing her.

"No," Jane replied softly, seductively. "I think I'll come to bed and say thank you, but I'll be bad, *very* bad," she whispered.

CHAPTER ELEVEN

Jane got a taxi and arrived at her parents' house on Christmas Eve laden down with presents. She had bought some in New York and spent her spare time searching for suitable gifts for the family. She had her own old room, the one she'd shared with Victoria when they were young. Somehow it was safe and comforting, like stepping back in time after the turmoil of the last few weeks.

Jack had returned to France, and they had arranged to keep in touch, but she would not be seeing him until sometime later in the New Year. She missed his company, his outgoing manner, his disruption of her life, and most of all his warm presence beside her in bed. Her mother was quick to notice a change in Jane.

"You've got lots of new clothes, and that hairstyle suits you. Have you got someone? You seem different."

Jane told her that she *was* seeing someone, but he was out of the country on business.

"Who is he? What does he do?" There was no putting her mother off once she'd scented the trail of a possible relationship.

"He's a horse breeder and trainer," Jane replied, that was as far as she was going to go at the moment.

"Horses? Where on earth did you meet him?" her mother gasped, surprised.

"He nearly knocked me over," Jane explained, enjoying the look on her mother's face.

"On a horse, where was that?" She was truly into her stride.

"Not a horse. A motor bike, near to my flat."

"Where does he keep them?" The

questions just kept rolling, and Jane decided to clear the air.

"The horses are in the country, in France, but he has an apartment in London where he also keeps two motor bikes. That's how it happened. Actually, I've moved into his apartment, but we still have to get things settled."

"He's married." It was a statement, not a question from her mother, and Jane was honest in her reply.

"Separated," she corrected. "We're sorting things out, but he's the one. I'm going to be with him."

She had expected more questions, but to her surprise, her mother let the subject go. She obviously needed time to digest the information she'd been given so far, but Jane knew that she could expect many more questions in the next couple of days.

§

Christmas Day was very traditional. Victoria and Julian arrived by late morning and everyone took their time opening their presents. Slippers, bottles of spirits, a cocktail shaker, books, scarves, make up and expensive toiletries all littered the room. Jane had taken the gift-wrapped package from Tiffany's downstairs and saved it to open last.

"Wow!" Victoria gasped when she saw the watch. She raised her eyebrows and caught Jane's glance.

As Jane fastened the fabulous watch onto her wrist, she realised that it was the first time she had ever seen her twin a little envious of her. It should have been a bit of a triumph, but instead all she felt was the absence of Jack. She remembered the upsetting scene in the hotel room about the present and was glad that they'd made things up between them before they left New York.

After an enormous Christmas dinner, the men offered to clear the table and stack the dishwasher, while Victoria, Jane and their mother collapsed into comfortable chairs.

"I'll never eat again!" Victoria said. It seemed that at last the sickness had gone and she was beginning to enjoy her food.

"What did you say this new man was called?" her mother asked and Jane knew that she would have to answer a few more questions.

"Jack Flynn," she replied. "He's married to a French woman, has a daughter and a business in France. He's spending Christmas with them, but we're going to be together when he's divorced."

She hoped she had covered everything.

"And is he going to marry you when he's free?"

It was a good question, and Jane wished she knew the answer herself.

§

Her mother had arranged for them all to stay for two nights; she enjoyed having the family together and wanted to give Victoria a rest. On Boxing Day everyone slept late, then went for a walk around the local park later in the morning. After lunch, another lazy afternoon followed. The TV was on, they talked about the arrival of the baby in a few months, and Julian and Alan played with the dog in the large garden.

"I'll make a curry from the rest of the turkey later," her mother decided. "After that we'll all be wanting something different."

The lazy day drifted into evening. There was a frost outside and the heating was turned up.

Once the curry was nearly ready, Jane laid the table and set out wine glasses, lit three large candles, moved a vase of roses to the centre and stepped back to admire her work – very tasteful. She arranged five chairs around the table, for Julian and Victoria, her mother and father and herself. *An odd number*, she thought. *Me, on my own, with two happy couples.*

There was a knock at the door.

"I'll get it," her father shouted from the kitchen, where he was looking for a corkscrew. Jane heard voices in the hall, then her father's head popped round the door.

"It's someone for you," he said.

It was Jack! There, in her parents' house, in an expensive dark, cashmere suit, white shirt and silk tie, impeccably dressed, his eyes shining, his hair tamed, and holding a couple of bottles. He handed them to her surprised father – port and brandy –

introduced himself, then stepped forward and took Jane in his arms.

It was impossible, unexpected, fantastic, and pure theatre: pure Jack Flynn. She found that she was trembling, it was almost too much, but he confidently kept his arms around her while he introduced himself to the family.

"Sorry to drop in like this," he said, "but I wanted to see Jane. I hope I'm not interrupting anything. I can make it short and just go soon ..." He was charm itself, and Jane felt her heart turn over.

"No, please stay, we're only having turkey curry. There's plenty, please join us!" Her mother was the first to recover and, always a good hostess, invited him to stay. Jane could see she was completely taken aback by his elegant appearance and easy manner, and naturally, she wanted to find out more about him.

Victoria slipped next to Jane as Jack turned to thank their mother for the offer.

"He's stunning," she whispered and Jane began to glow.

The meal was the highlight of Christmas. The curry was delicious, the wine flowed, and Jack fitted in perfectly. He answered her mother's questions about Ireland, talked to her father about golf and professed an interest in garden design with Julian. He asked Victoria how she was feeling and even mentioned the birth of his own daughter.

Jane watched on in awe.

This was the best present she could have hoped for. He stretched out his hand and stroked her wrist, fondling the watch. Their eyes met and they shared their secret, the fiery argument over the present, the passion afterwards.

They moved to the lounge, everyone relaxing. Apart from Victoria, they were all drinking, and the time was passing too quickly. Jane wanted Jack to herself and wondered how she was going to manage it.

Eventually, Victoria announced that she was tired and would have to go to bed, and it seemed that the evening was drawing to a close.

"How did you get here?" Jane's father asked Jack.

"I drove."

"Then we must get you a taxi. Collect

your car tomorrow, you can't risk driving."

"Oh no," her mother interrupted. "I'm
sure we could put you up for the night ..."
She hesitated. "There's a couch in the
dining room, and I could find some
blankets."

Jack stood. "Thank you very much, Mrs
Harkness," he said. "I'll take you up on the
kind offer. But don't worry about bedding, I
won't put you to any trouble."

He held out his hand to Jane and pulled
her up from her seat. "I'll just sleep with
Jane."

§

"If you don't stop giggling I'll have to gag
you," Jack said, rolling over in the single
bed, holding her tight.

"I can't help it! My mother's face when
you said you'd sleep with me!"

"Well, you're not a child anymore. You
can decide to have a friend for a sleep-over,"
he joked. "Okay, we could have got a taxi
and gone back to my apartment, but it's
cosy here."

"I just can't believe you're here. What

happened?" she asked.

"Claudine's mother came, and they wanted to have time alone to talk about the future. So I took the chance that I would find you. I wanted to surprise you, but I've got to fly back tomorrow. I just wanted to see you."

Jane had never felt so wanted, so loved, even though it would only be for one night.

"Can you manage to keep quiet if I make wild love to you?" Jack asked. "I don't want your family to hear."

"I'll try."

Gag me, put the pillow over my face, cover my mouth with kisses, but please don't stop, she thought, *my wonderful, sexy Christmas present.*

CHAPTER TWELVE

Was is possible to love too much, Jane wondered.

The weeks after Christmas were difficult. Jack was back in France and travelling further abroad, making final arrangements, seeing lawyers, settling business. She missed him and tried to fill her days with extra hours at the cafe and helping Victoria at the large house in Wimbledon. She loved the apartment overlooking the river Thames, but it wasn't the same on her own. Jack made a few hurried visits, sweeping her off her feet, filling her with excitement, then disappearing back to France.

"How can you arrange flights at such short notice?" she asked, as he flung his minimum items into an overnight bag, ready to go again. He kept the extensive wardrobes and cupboards at the apartment filled with his extra clothes, so that he could travel lightly.

There was a short pause before he spoke. She hardly ever asked about his life away from her, and there were times when she really didn't want to think about it.

"We have a private plane, the Company I mean," he said. Jane was stunned, she knew he was wealthy, but even so – she had never imagined *private planes.*

"And a yacht, too? Villa in Tuscany? Ski Lodge?" Suddenly she needed to know.

Jack turned and took her in his arms.

"All those and more. When everything is settled, I'll take you wherever in the world you want to go."

Jane held him tightly. "I just want to be with *you*," she said. "Anywhere will do."

"Be patient a little longer. Trust me, Jane."

They said goodbye. She had noticed that Jack had lost a little weight: he was leaner and harder, as though he had been working out, and there were shadows under his brilliant blue eyes. She knew then that he was dismantling his life in France, which must be a strain. And it was for her!

"I won't be back for a while. There are some financial arrangements to be finalised in Switzerland, but I'll keep in touch."

Again, he was gone.

§

Jane was at Victoria's house, for her usual Friday housework routine. She had restored the rooms to order and felt that there had been a welcome change in her relationship with her twin. In a few months the baby would arrive, Julian would arrange for a full time au pair or nanny, and she would no longer be needed.

She sat on the bed in the master bedroom. Perhaps, by that time, she would be with Jack: they would be living together in London and thinking about their own future. He still talked about a life in the countryside, with horses, dogs and children. The thought filled her with joy. She had been tempted to abandon the pill, take a chance on becoming pregnant, start the process of trying to build the family he wanted, but something held her back. It would be rushing things. She had only known him for six months and already their lives were turned upside-down.

Idly, she reached over and took a glossy magazine from Victoria's dresser. She always had loads of the latest issues and spent time browsing through them, planning her look for when she was no longer restricted to maternity clothes. Jane flicked through, past the fashion, beauty, glitzy social events, and then ...

She caught her breath.

There on the page was *Jack*, dazzling in tuxedo and white tie, accompanied by a tall, chic, dark woman, beautifully dressed in a long, black designer dress, sparkling with diamonds. Claudine. She read the blurb. It was a New Year's Ball, held in Dublin at the exclusive newly restored hotel and spa owned by the French Consortium. The opening had been attended by all the smart, rich people in Dublin, along with many celebrities who had flown in especially for the event.

Choking, she checked the date. There was no mistake, it was this New Year.

The night she had refused all invitations from friends and sat alone in the apartment, listening to Big Ben striking midnight, he had been with Claudine. He was still carrying on his life with her, and only a week after they had made frantic love in her bedroom at her parents' house at Christmas.

Stumbling down the stairs, Jane grabbed her handbag and rang for a taxi. She leant against the wall in the kitchen, overwhelmed with shock. He had told her he was busy winding up his financial affairs, when in reality he had been attending a ball with Claudine in Dublin.

The thought turned over and over in her mind. She had trusted him. How many other times had he been out socialising with his separated wife whilst she waited alone for him?

In a daze she let herself into the apartment, and sat down overlooking the river. At last she could let herself cry.

She sat through the night, until the first rays of light appeared over the city, weeping alone, then she packed all her belongings. She wrote a short note and propped it up on the coffee table. She didn't go into details, just said that she was leaving, and that she could no longer live there.

Then she contacted Victoria and asked if she could stay for a while, just a temporary arrangement and was relieved that her twin agreed without any questions, sensing that she needed a refuge.

§

For the next week, Jane worked longer at the cafe, staying after hours to clean up, trying to exhaust herself and clear her mind. Eventually, over a glass of wine, she told Victoria what had happened.

"Are you sure?" Victoria asked. "There could be some other explanation. I thought he was the one."

"So did I," Jane murmured.

She kept her mobile phone switched off and used the land-line at the cafe. The days passed in a blur of work, heading back to eat with Victoria and Julian, then early nights, lying awake in the guest room. She was tempted to take a bottle of wine to bed with her, but resisted drinking alone. Her life was at a standstill. She missed Jack desperately, but tried to push her memories away. Only time would perhaps heal her wounded heart.

§

Julian had collected Thai take away on the way home. They sat around the large kitchen table, Victoria with a glass of water and Julian and Jane sharing a bottle of cold Chablis.

"I'll really have to sort myself out, I can't keep living here with you," Jane said.

Julian remained silent, probably relieved that the subject had been raised. Jane sensed that he was more than ready to return to his ordered life with Victoria.

"There's no rush," Victoria assured her, sipping her water slowly. "Stay as long as you need."

What about the future? Jane wondered to herself. *What would life be like without Jack?*

There was an insistent ringing of the front

door bell.

"I'll get it," Jane offered. She felt that the silence around the table had become awkward and that it meant that Julian really *was* getting tired of her continued presence.

She unlocked the heavy front door and felt it pushed roughly wide. Jack strode into the hallway, his eyes blazing and anger radiating from him.

"What the hell is this?" he said, waving her note in the air.

"I'm staying here, it's over," she replied, amazed that her voice sounded so firm.

"No discussion, no explanation, just like that?" His voice was raised, and Jane became aware that Julian and Victoria were standing in the doorway at the end of the hall. They had obviously heard the noise.

"You told me that you were separated, winding things up, and all the time you were out with your wife," she countered.

Jane knew that she had put the magazine with the photograph of New Year on the shelf in the kitchen. She pushed past Victoria and returned with it in her hands, found the page and thrust it at him.

"New Year, which I spent on my own,

while you were at a ball in Dublin with
Claudine."

Jack glanced at the page.

"Of course we were together then," he
said quietly. "It was business. The opening
of the first of the company's Spas in Ireland,
we had been working on it for over a year
and promised a big opening night. It had
been arranged months ago – even before I
met you."

Jack snatched the magazine from her
hand and roughly ripped it in two, throwing
the pieces on the floor.

"I asked you to trust me, Jane, but
obviously that's hard for you." His furious
voice filled the room.

"Now hang on a minute ..." Julian said.

"Keep out of this," Jack snapped, whirling
round to face him, and Jane was afraid he
would order Julian out of his own hallway.

Instead he reached into his inside pocket
and took out an envelope which he tossed
onto the hall table.

"You can open this when I've gone," he
said. "Decide what you want to do."

He turned and went out, slamming the
front door behind him.

There was a stunned silence in the house, and then they heard the sound of a car door slamming and the roar of an engine. He had gone.

Jane found that she was shaking. She was usually a fairly peaceful person. She wasn't used to such scenes: shouting, ripping up things, slamming doors. Oh, what had she done?

Victoria was the first to recover. She picked up the envelope and put her arm around her twin.

"Give us a while, Julian, we're just going upstairs to sort this out," she said, guiding Jane up the stairs and leading her to the guest room. They sat on the bed, the envelope on the duvet between them.

"Well, are you going to open it, or sit there all night?" Victoria said, back to her usual organising self, but somehow, surprisingly, Jane found it comforting. Slowly she reached for the envelope and opened it, taking out the contents.

"What is it, let me see?" Victoria said.

"A plane ticket," Jane replied, "to Cork, for next Saturday. That's all, nothing else in there."

Victoria took the ticket, read it, then put it down carefully on the bed.

"He wanted to take you to Ireland," she exclaimed. "Back to his roots ... Maybe even to meet his mother!"

"And I've ruined it," Jane wailed. "He was so angry." She looked over at her twin and amazed to see that her eyes were sparkling.

"But he *was* pretty magnificent, wasn't he? Throwing things around ... Shouting at Julian ..." She began to giggle as Jane watched in surprise.

"But why didn't he tell me about New Year?"

"Would you have understood? Be honest," Victoria replied.

"What can I do?" Jane sighed.

Victoria turned towards her, and held her hand.

"You really don't have much idea about men, do you?" she said. "He loves you, otherwise why would he get so agitated – bursting in here like a rampaging stallion. Oh Jane, he was so passionate. I'd give anything for someone to feel like that about me."

"But you have Julian ..."

"Yes, he's a good husband and he'll be a good father. But what you'll have is more than that. He's so hotblooded, so full of life, such excitement ..."

"It's not easy," Jane replied.

"Who wants *easy*?" Victoria was on a roll now.

Jane considered what Victoria had been saying: it was true that she didn't feel confident around   men. She worried about her size, her lack of style, her comparison against other women. But Jack had told her that he wanted her as she was, no changes, just for herself.

"I've made a terrible mistake, haven't I?" she admitted.

"Just give him time to cool off. We can put that right."

Jane heard the old, organising tone in Victoria's voice, and for the first time, she welcomed it.

"First, I'll take a week's leave from work. We'll go shopping, get you some new clothes. I mean, you've let yourself go a bit lately. Not designer labels, nothing too sexy. Jack likes you quite feminine and simply dressed, but we can spend money on the cut and the fabrics. Second, we'll both go to that Spa you liked, for a couple of days. Maybe even stay the night. I could do with a bit of pampering myself." She stopped to take a breath.

"But that must be so expensive!" Jane cut in.

"It obviously belongs to him. So use the credit card he gave you. After all, it will just be transferring money from one of his accounts to another."

Jane let the idea wash over her. She began to feel hope; what Victoria was saying made sense.

"Finally, you'll get on that plane to Cork. You'll go through the doors at the other end, all tranquil, pampered, looking great, and you'll knock his socks off."

They began to laugh. It was partly relief and, for Jane, almost hysteria, as they fell backwards onto the bed, the precious plane ticket lying there between them.

When they'd recovered, Victoria rolled over towards her twin and spoke softly.

"Just a bit of advice ... When you see him, no recriminations, no grovelling, don't go over this night again. Just start afresh. And one more thing? Get him into bed as soon as you can."

Jane thought that she would have no problem with that.

CHAPTER THIRTEEN

The plane was slightly delayed. Jane had ordered a gin and tonic on board to try to calm her nerves. She knew that she looked good – a soft grey, silk jersey shift dress, which just skimmed her curves, a pale blue cashmere jacket, black tights and black shoes, with heels higher than she usually managed, plus a chunky silver necklace and ear-rings. Simple, elegant, nothing flashy. The time at the Spa with Victoria had been heaven, and now she was almost ready to face Jack.

She strolled through the airport lounge, trailing her new suitcase on wheels, and looked around. Where *was* he?

She checked her watch: the plane had been fifteen minutes late. Surely he would have arrived by now? An uneasy feeling began to grow in the pit of her stomach. Something just didn't feel right. He had changed his mind. He hadn't meant her to come after the awful scene at Victoria's house. She walked towards the doors; maybe he was outside.

"Jane?" A voice behind her.

She turned. Not Jack, but a woman: an exquisitely dressed woman in black, very French looking.

"I'm Claudine," she said, moving towards Jane. "Can you come with me? I have a car outside."

In a daze, Jane followed her out to a large black Mercedes, with a driver waiting to help them in. She sat down on the back seat and looked at Jack's wife – his ex-wife or estranged wife. Which was it?

"I'm sorry to tell you, but there's been an accident."

The car started up and began to roll slowly, smoothly away from the airport.

"Jack?" Jane gasped in horror. *Please no,*

no, not that.

"He's alive, but injured." Claudine paused. "Spinal problems. At the moment, he's paralysed from the waist down."

Jane felt herself go clammy as the words sank in. Dazed with shock she tried to breathe slowly, to fully understand what Claudine was saying.

"An accident on his motor bike?" The words tumbled from her mouth; nothing made sense to her.

"No, a horse," Claudine replied, turning towards her. "He has a lot of cuts and bruises, minor injuries which don't really matter. But you have to face it, there's a possibility that he may not walk again."

There was a silence as Jane tried to take in the dreadful news. The car stopped in a quiet road not far from the airport.

"It happened four days ago. I tried to have him transferred to America for treatment, but he refused. He's in a little country hospital some miles away. I've had specialists flown in to see him, a room equipped with all special aids. He'll have the best care I can arrange, but there isn't any guarantee that it will work."

She paused, letting the words sink in.

"He told me to send you away."

"Away? Why?" Jane asked, distraught.

"Because he might not recover. He doesn't want to be a burden to you."

"I'm not going away," Jane said, slumping back in the car, as Claudine gently took her hand.

"Be sure. Think it over carefully. That's why I had the car stop here. You can get back on a plane, leave if you want to, and he won't blame you. It's a big decision."

"I'm staying," Jane said, steadying herself as she looked at the older woman. "This is my life choice, whatever happens."

A small smile appeared on Claudine lips; she tapped the window to let the driver know they were carrying on with the journey.

"I'm glad he met you," she said. "He's had lots of girls in the last couple of years who would have run away at the first sign of trouble. They were just after the glamour and the money."

§

At last the car pulled up at the entrance to the small country hospital. Claudine stayed where she was as the driver opened the door on Jane's side.

"I'm not coming in with you," she explained. "He'll be angry that I've brought you here. You'll be better on your own with him. Can you handle it?"

Jane nodded, but her legs were trembling as she crossed towards the entrance. She must be strong. She was going stay, whatever he said. Life had just dropped another bombshell and she must face up to it.

A young nurse guided her through the corridors. She stopped and gently pushed a door open.

"I think he's asleep," she whispered.

Jane looked around: a large, pale cream room, white blinds at the windows, and tasteful pictures of country scenes on the walls. She concentrated on the surroundings, anywhere except the bed. The large, steel framed, hospital bed and Jack, half covered by a white blanket, tubes and drips attached to his body. Slowly, quietly, she moved towards him, trying to breathe deeply to control her anxiety and fear of the situation. His eyes opened and he looked at her. Those piercing, fantastic, blue eyes held hers, assessing her, as she tried to gauge his reaction.

"I told Claudine to send you away," he said.

"Well she didn't, and I wouldn't have gone anyway." Jane quietly stood her ground.

Jack put his hand up and ran it through his hair, it was longer than usual, more curly.

"Why don't I ever meet women who do as they're told?" he asked.

"Oh, such an out-dated idea! I'm surprised at you."

Jane moved towards the bed, leaned down and brushed the hair from his eyes. Slowly, gently, she kissed the cut above his left eye, the bruises on his cheeks, the stubble on his chin.

"Did Claudine tell you everything? You know the outlook might not be good. I didn't want you to feel you have to stay with me."

"Yes, I know that and I'm not changing

my mind." Jane tried to concentrate on his
face as she spoke, not on the medical
equipment attached to his body. "I'm not
someone who's here just for the good times,
Jack. I want to stay with you and help you. If
you have to go around the world trying
different treatments, then I'll be there.
There isn't any way that I'm going to leave
you now."

"Oh, Jane, I think I've loved you since
that night you stepped out in front my bike,"
Jack said, taking her hand and holding it
tightly.

"You almost knocked me over."

"You didn't look where you were going."

"You were riding too fast."

She pulled up a chair and sat beside the
bed. They held hands, and a peaceful
silence descended. She could tell he was
exhausted, but she didn't want to let go of
his warm, strong hand.

"What were you doing here, in Ireland?"
she asked.

"Looking at a horse I might buy, among
other things. You need to know, the
financial settlement is made. We've split
everything. Claudine has the beauty

business, the chateau, and the apartment in Paris."

"You don't need to tell me all this now," Jane interrupted.

"I want to," he continued. "It's time. I have the apartment in London, the horses, the racing stables, and we both have more money than we could ever spend in a lifetime. Oh, and then there are the holiday homes ..."

"Stop, really, *please*. It's too much." Jane looked away. She wasn't ready to think about his wealth just yet.

"I left this country as a penniless drifter and I've returned a millionaire," he said quietly. "Who would have thought it?"

He pressed a button beside him and the top half of the bed raised slowly, enabling him to sit up.

"If you're sure you're staying, I'm going to make some conditions."

Jane nodded. She was too emotionally wrung-out to object.

"They do all the medical work on me in the mornings – so don't come then. I don't want you to see it. Just appear in the afternoons, after I've had a rest. I'll look forward to it. Okay?"

"Yes," Jane answered.

"I've got my phone and laptop here. I'll book you into a great hotel not far away, and there'll be a car and driver available for you. Get out in the mornings. Explore, enjoy yourself, find things to do. Then you can tell me all about it later."

She knew he would like to organise these arrangements for her; it would give him a purpose, take his mind off the pain, something other than his hospital treatment to concentrate on.

"Whatever you say," she replied.

Jack raised his eyebrows and gave her a searching look.

"Well, that's a start," he said.

§

It worked well for the first couple of weeks. Jack had booked her a suite at a luxury hotel a few miles away, and the driver, Sean, was ready each morning to take her wherever she fancied going. It was just Spring, and they drove down narrow lanes between misty fields, damp hedgerows brushing the sides of the car, stopping at villages on the way. Jack booked activities for her: art galleries to visit, small theatres in the evenings, even cookery lessons. She had objected at first.

"I can't cook!"

"Exactly, you need to learn," he replied with a grin.

"I don't know if I'm that interested," she continued.

"If we're going to live right out in the country, there won't be any supermarkets down the road with ready meals, or any take aways," he responded.

She gave in. Living in the country! He was planning for the future, for when he was able to leave hospital. It was a positive sign.

She tried to occupy her mornings and appear fresh in the afternoons at the hospital, ready to talk, ready to be bright and entertaining.

But sometimes it was exhausting in spite of her best intentions. He could be pale, tired and edgy, and she knew that the extensive treatments were wearing. He pushed himself to respond to whatever new remedies were tried. Yet, most times, he was overwhelmingly pleased to see her, ready to listen and asking all sorts of questions about her mornings. She tried to keep positive, too. She was desperate to see some improvement, wondering if he would walk again.

Then they had their first row since she had arrived in Ireland. She had gone into his room, full of news, eager to tell him what she had arranged herself, expecting a good response.

"I've booked myself some riding lessons at the local stables," she said.

There was an ominous pause.

"*Riding* lessons? Why? And which stable? Give me the name."

"Flanagan's. I'm going tomorrow."

"Not until I've spoken to them, given them some instructions," he stated.

"What instructions?" she asked. "I'm the one who is going for a lesson!" She felt disappointed, at end of her patience; it wasn't the reaction she had expected.

"And *I'm* the one who's paying. I'll tell them what to provide, and how to teach you."

Jane was stunned. Why was he trying to control her like this? She loved him and wanted to be able to ride with him if he was ever got on a horse again. She had thought he'd be pleased. She was afraid that she was going to cry. She felt so emotional lately, and tried to hold the tears back; she wasn't going to let him see.

There was an atmosphere in the room now, neither of them was willing to break the extended, frosty silence.

To her relief the door opened. Claudine stood there, and with her a little girl, skinny and small for her age, with short dark hair and Jack's unmistakeable brilliant blue eyes.

"Papa!" she cried.

She raced across the room and threw herself on the bed, clinging to him, speaking rapidly in French. He held her tight, stroking her hair, kissing her cheeks and answering her fluently in her own language. Jane felt choked. She rose and joined Claudine in the doorway.

"I'll give you some space," she said.

"You look a little pale, are you all right?" Claudine asked. She had followed Jane into the corridor.

"Can we talk?" Jane needed to confide in someone who might understand, and who better than Jack's ex-wife?

"Come outside," Claudine replied, "there are some benches."

They sat in the watery sun and Jane told Claudine everything: about the arrangements he insisted on making for her, his unpredictable temperament, her own guilt at enjoying herself whilst he was confined to a hospital bed, and then the final blow-up about her idea of riding lessons.

"Well, I can understand about the riding. He's concerned for your safety. Let that one go until he's checked it out."

Jane nodded.

"It's not going to be easy," Claudine continued. "He's frustrated, restless, desperate to be walking and out of here. He just wants to be soothed in the afternoons when he sees you. Maybe even provide a little special distraction, let me think about that."

Jane leaned back on the bench, letting the sun warm her face, trying to calm down.

To her surprise, Claudine sat forward,

covering her face with her hands.

"I still love him, you know," she said quietly. "I'm not actually *in love* but he is the father of my child. When I met him he was so young, so carefree. I encouraged him to be a successful business man. We made a great team and he turned the Consortium around. He could charm the birds off the trees at the same time as striking a hard deal. He's spent years flying all around the world, living in the fast lane, but his heart was always here. Where he is now, in what he calls 'The Old Country'. And now he doesn't know if he'll ever walk again. You can understand that he must be raging inside."

Jane felt miserable and selfish. She loved Jack, so why couldn't she understand this man as Claudine seemed to.

"I would suggest a little distraction, liven up the afternoons," Claudine said, leaning forward. "Provide some fun. If you *do* have a riding lesson, appear in your jodhpurs and riding boots, straight from your lesson, smelling of the stables. That should shake him up. Then, the next day, all glamour, sophistication."

"I don't really do sophisticated," Jane sighed.

"Well, your version then; the day after, something different. Think up some sexy ideas. He'll be waiting for that door to open, not knowing what's coming next. A little theatre, that's all. Keep him guessing."

For the first time in her life Jane wished that she had been born in France instead of London.

Claudine stood and stretched.

"We came on the company plane. I've brought a Swiss doctor with me. He's had good results with people injured in skiing accidents. His methods are new, unconventional. He'll stay a while, do some more tests, have a look at the situation. Would you like a break? You could come back with us? I could take you shopping in Paris or you can rest at the chateau?"

Jane shook her head. "Thanks but no, my place is here."

§

She went back quietly into Jack's room. Claudine and Amelie had left, and she could see that he was fighting his fatigue.

"I'll go now," she said gently. "I just came to say goodbye."

He held out his hand to her.

"Sorry about giving you a hard time. I just get so frustrated being here."

Jane took his hand and held it in both of hers – his hard, strong hand that had so tenderly stroked and held his daughter.

"It's okay," she said. "We'll be fine, Jack. We'll get through this together."

CHAPTER FOURTEEN

While the Swiss doctor carried out yet more tests, Jane took a day off from hospital visiting and got Sean to drive her to Dublin. She hit the shops, spending more than she had ever imagined. Riding gear – the whole expensive bag – boutiques, classy clothes, sexy underwear, stockings with lacy tops, suspender belts, and, at the end of the exciting day, a simple linen and silk shift dress. It would be for the summer, perhaps to wear if he came out of hospital. Back at the hotel suite she tried them all on, spreading them across the large bed, amazed at her mad fling. Would Jack ever query the amount she put on the credit card he had given her, she wondered. After all, he kept telling her to use it but she was still shocked at the total.

Flanagan's Riding Stables had been approved and she had her first lesson. Mr Flanagan stood in the yard, holding the reins of a small, docile white horse.

"I have my instructions from Mr Flynn himself," he said. "I'm to take things slowly, and stay with you all the time. No getting ahead of yourself and cantering off now."

He smiled at her and Jane grinned back. They understood each other; Jack was obviously on the case.

She found riding harder than she had expected and later ached more than she had ever experienced. Still, she kept it up, booking lessons in the mornings for the next few days. She was determined to learn and soon began to enjoy it.

§

Jane opened the door into Jack's room and stopped for a moment in the doorway. She had taken Claudine's advice and gone straight from her riding lesson: in jodhpurs which stretched tightly across her ample thighs and polished, black riding boots, a silky shirt with the top two buttons undone and a jacket tossed casually around her shoulders.

She waited for his reaction.

To her surprise, he just glanced up casually from his newspaper. "Good lesson?" he asked.

"Great," she replied. "Sorry, I lost track of the time. I just rushed straight here."

He shrugged. "That shows you're doing well."

Jane strolled across to the bed and kissed him. She was aware of a strong smell of horse which she had brought into the sterile room. She waited for some comment, but he didn't appear to notice the aroma, and she began to feel embarrassed that she hadn't showered before she arrived.

"Are you going to sit down, or have you got to dash off?" He asked, looking at her teasingly, but there was something else in his eyes, and she couldn't work it out. Surprise? Amusement? A flicker of annoyance?

They passed the afternoon as usual, talking, holding hands, swapping information. She wasn't sure if she had carried out her performance *quite* as planned and decided on a different approach the next day ...

A black dress with high neckline, long sleeves, but in a soft material which clung to her body, emphasising her shape, her curves, and stopping just above her knees, with a slit up the side. She wore suspenders, black, with lacy topped stockings and stiletto heels. She had bathed, blow dried her hair and applied her make up carefully, a spray of expensive perfume.

But suddenly she was plagued by doubts as she stood outside the door to the hospital room. Was it right, she wondered. Was it even fair? She was dressed like something from an arty French film and he was paralysed from the waist down. Perhaps it was cruel, even.

Breathing in deeply, she turned the handle and entered.

Jack was sitting up, playing a game on his laptop.

"Nice and early today," he said. Again no

mention of her appearance.

Jane crossed the room and pulled up a visitors' chair close to the bed, angling it towards him. Slowly, she sat down and crossed her legs. He watched her carefully. He had seen the top of her lacy, black stockings – just a glimpse – she knew he had! She had practised it before the mirror in her hotel room.

He raised an eyebrow.

"Have you been to cookery lessons today?" he asked quietly.

§

She couldn't do the show any more; it just wasn't her and she didn't have the expertise to carry it off. The next day she took the cream shift dress from the wardrobe and tried it on. Simple, beautifully cut, with a round neck, sleeveless and skimming her body, ending at the knees. She put on the watch that Jack had bought her in New York and brushed her hair into a sleek, glossy shape. It was more comfortable, the day was warmer and she tried on some sandals and a cashmere cardigan in a delicate shade of pink.

Her spirits rose, there was a promise of something in the air.

Pushing the door open happily, Jane stepped into the hospital room. Jack looked up. Again he had been using his laptop.

"Wait," he said. "Stop right there for a moment. Ah, yes, today I see that we have Miss Harkness back."

Jane hesitated in the doorway, unsure whether he was joking or not.

"Come here," he said, holding out his hand. "I was wondering what you would devise today."

"Oh, dear ..." Jane mumbled.

"It's been very entertaining, very amusing, very ... *French*?" He was definitely teasing her.

She went across and stood by the bed.

"I was just trying to surprise you, liven up your day," she explained.

"Take that cardigan thing off and let me hold you."

His arms went round her, stroking her body.

"You don't need to do that," he continued. "I keep telling you that I love you, just the way you are. All of you."

"Sorry, it was a mistake." Jane felt a little subdued.

"The stockings were nice though," he said, his voice low, his hands pulling her down to sit on the bed.

He was different, elated even, and Jane began to think that perhaps her little performances *had* worked some sort of magic after all.

"What's this?"

He had found the zip which went down the back of her dress, and he gently turned her round on the bed so that she had her back to him.

"If I undo this a little, I can kiss your neck ..."

She felt the zip slowly slide down, and sure enough, he kissed the back of her neck. Jane shivered with pleasure. A little further, so gently, the zip was eased down and deliciously he kissed her back, his warm fingers exploring.

"White lace, very pretty. And what about the rest, under there? *More* lace?"

Jane nodded, as he opened the back of her dress even further.

"If I take this right down to the bottom, you can stand up and your dress will fall off. Let me see you, Jane."

She was finding it difficult to breathe. Her thoughts were tumbling around and her body was responding to his touch.

"We're in a hospital, Jack!" she managed to gasp.

"Take a chance," he smiled. "You've been provoking me all week. Don't go shy on me now."

He was reckless, impulsive, insistent, but she needed him, and she would do it, whatever he wanted.

"Mr Flynn!"

Just then, the door was flung open and Sister Brennan stood in the doorway, her stout body encased in her immaculate uniform, glasses perched on her nose, bristling with indignation.

"There is a *horse-box* in the grounds of my hospital and I believe you arranged it."

"Ah, yes, Sister, let me explain..."

Jane felt him slowly trying to zip up her dress as he spoke.

"No explanations please. I would never have allowed it, but the powers above say you can go outside for a while."

She stood aside and a young nurse pushed a wheelchair into the room. Together they transferred him into the chair whilst Jane stood beside the bed.

"Fifteen minutes and no more, and I'll be staying with you," Sister Brennan said, grasping the handles and starting to push Jack towards the door.

"Nurse," the Sister added, glancing over her shoulder, "help Miss Harkness with her dress. She seems to be having some difficulty."

Jane heard Jack try to stifle a snort of laughter as they left the room.

§

"Just look at him, isn't he the most magnificent beast," Jack said, his eyes shining.

The horse was the colour of burnished copper, huge, terrifying, lurching around, as the groom held grimly onto his bridle, kicking his heels, swishing his black tail, tossing his head. Jane even thought that she could see his eyes rolling.

"I've made up my mind. I'm having him, not even negotiating any more." Jack was on a high.

Any more? Jane thought.

"You've seen him before? Don't tell me he's the one that threw you!"

Jane felt an icy wave of terror begin to creep through her as he turned and looked directly into her eyes.

"Yes," Jack admitted. "He's high spirited, difficult, but wonderful breeding stock, too. The start of my new bloodline. At the moment, he's confused, temperamental, and doesn't know what's happening to him or where he is. But he just needs to know that he *belongs* to me, to trust me, and I can settle him."

He was holding her hand and at this, he squeezed it tightly.

"You know I can do that, don't you, Jane?"

Yes, she did. And he would. She knew that he wasn't only speaking of the stallion.

Sister Brennan had relaxed her grip on the wheelchair and Jack propelled it slightly forwards.

"I'm going a little nearer," he said. "But

just me. Any more people will spook him."

Jane held her breath as he approached the horse, slowly, quietly. She expected him to stop a few metres away, but he rolled on, across the grass, right next to the excitable animal. He stretched out a hand and stroked the quivering flanks and Jane was aware that he was speaking in a soft murmur. At any moment the horse might lash out, overturning the wheelchair, trampling Jack, kicking his head. She closed her eyes, unable to watch any more.

"Will you just look at that!" Sister Brennan exclaimed.

Jack had rolled back towards the horse's tossing head. As the groom held on to the rein, he reached up and caressed the long neck, still speaking in low tones. He leaned his head against the horse's neck and gave some signal to the groom to drop the bridle.

Jane could hardly bear to watch, as the animal stood alone, unleashed. He could rear up, gallop off. What in the world was Jack thinking of?

The minutes passed, and Jack continued to talk to the horse, stroking him gently. Then the prancing stopped, and a stillness came over the huge animal and slowly he lowered his great head towards Jack, nuzzling his shoulder.

§

The little procession returned to the hospital room. Jack was happier than he had been for days, Sister Brennan was confounded, and Jane still hadn't stopped shaking.

"There we are, Mr Flynn," the Sister said. "Do you want to stay in the chair for a while and is there anything more I can do for you now?" she asked returning to her firm manner.

"Just one thing, please Sister," Jack said, looking at Jane, making her hold his glance, his eyes alive with life. "Can you see if there's a doctor around, as I need to speak to one. When I was outside just now I felt a small tingle in my toes. It may be nothing, but that's the second time something has stirred today."

CHAPTER FIFTEEN

There was an air of suppressed excitement in the car. Jack was elated, but refused to tell Jane why or where they were heading. He was out for the whole day! Out of hospital, using elbow crutches to get around slowly, with Sean driving the large, black Mercedes, and on hand to help.

Jane gazed out of the window, at lush fields, a little mist hanging over the hedgerows.

"Just give me a clue," she asked. "Where on earth are we?"

"Kerry, the beautiful West," was all he would say.

She lounged back contentedly. Three weeks of intense exercises and treatment, since that first tingle of feeling had returned, and now he was almost ready to leave the hospital. He would have to return for a while for check ups, and further physiotherapy, but he would be out, and for the time being would move into the country hotel with her. He had even persuaded Sister Brennan to let him out the day before their excursion.

"Just to check out the hotel room, Sister," he had said, avoiding Jane's eye, "in case there are any special aids I might need."

The bed, the high, soft bed in the luxurious hotel suite. Gradually, he made his way over and patted it, testing the surface. It was the middle of the morning.

"I might need a bit of help getting out of these clothes," he said, looking at her with a playful smile. "What do you think, shall we give it a go?"

"Not a very romantic way to put it, after all this time," Jane replied, putting her arms around his waist, careful not to unbalance him.

He leaned down and kissed the top of her

head.

"Your back," she said. "You will have to be careful...."

"Of course."

But he wasn't, and it was great.

§

Whilst Jack was still recovering in the hospital, Victoria had had a little boy. It had been an emergency; he was early and Victoria was rushed to the maternity ward. Afterwards, Jack had insisted that Jane should use the private plane to fly to London and she had accepted gratefully.

She had cuddled her little nephew, listened to Victoria's account of the whole birth, and drunk many cups of tea provided by their mother, who had moved herself in to help for a few days.

Jane let herself drift off, and looked around the nursery, newly painted, full of the clutter of baby equipment, presents for the tiny boy strewn around.

This is what I've been jealous of, she thought, as she finally faced the thought. Only last year, she had wanted what

Victoria had – the detached house in Wimbledon, the two cars, the husband with a well-paid, settled job and a secure future. Instead, she had Jack, pushing himself to exhaustion to walk again, restless, challenging, impatient for his divorce to be finalised. But, at the same time, tender, loving, filling her with such unexpected joy.

Out of the blue, a picture came into her mind: Jack, with his own daughter, stroking and comforting Amelie as she had clung to him in distress.

"Sorry?"

Jane was suddenly aware that Victoria had asked a question.

"I said, how is that gorgeous Irishman?" Victoria queried.

"Fine, just fine," Jane replied.

§

The car slowed and turned left through a stone arch, down a track; a driveway with grass growing in the middle. Emerging from the trees, just bathed in the watery sun, was a castle.

A small castle, with towers, battlements,

and thick stone walls, sitting in a meadow of wild flowers. Gentle hills rose in the background and Jane looked around in wonder as the car stopped and she got out.

"It's beautiful," she admired.

Sean helped Jack to negotiate the step from the car and handed over his crutches.

"Isn't it!" agreed Jack. "It needs a lot of renovation, of course, and money spending on it, but that's no problem. Look at the view, the pastures. There's even a farm on the estate, with dairy cows, and also a courtyard at the back, and stables ... So? What do you think?" he asked, happily gazing around.

"You're going to buy it, and turn it into a spa?" Jane replied.

She thought it would take some time and a huge amount of investment, but would be a fantastic location. She also thought that he was no longer involved in that part of the business.

"No, not a spa," Jack said. "It's for us, if you like it. That's the reason I wanted you to come to Ireland, to see it. Have a look around. It's a wonderful place, and not too isolated, either. There's a village a few miles away. I know it looks a bit neglected now, but some of the rooms are sound. You can have them restored any way you want, no expense spared, and the stables won't take too long to get into shape."

"A castle! You want us to live in a castle?" Jane felt dizzy at the thought.

"Only if *you* like it. Marry me, Jane. We can do it up together, settle here, and have lots of horses, dogs, and children." He was so enthusiastic and eager to share his ideas, as he leaned against the stone wall.

"No," she replied.

"No?"

There was a pause.

"You don't like it?" Jack asked, a look of astonishment on his face. "Or you won't marry me?"

"Yes, or I mean, no," Jane continued struggle ng trying to find the right words. "I love it, and I love you. I do want to be with you. I know how much you love Amelie, but you've got your priorities wrong just now, Jack. Always the horses first, then dogs, and lastly *our* children."

There was a stillness in the air between them as he considered her answer. The only sound Jane could hear were birds singing and the distant lowing of a cow. He remained silent, and she felt a flutter of anxiety in her pounding heart. Had she pushed too far, and risked everything?

He tried to straighten up, and as he did so, she was afraid to look him in the eyes.

"I'll ask you again," he said in a low, serious voice, "but only once."

Jane gulped.

"Look at me," he ordered. "Miss Harkness ... when I'm free, will you marry me, and live here with me in this beautiful, remote corner of Ireland? Will you let me look after you and trust that I love you? And together, we can have lots of children, if we are lucky, *and* horses and dogs."

His eyes, usually so brilliantly blue, and crinkling with laughter lines at the corners, were now unreadable pools of darkness.

Jane stepped towards him and reached up to put her arms around his neck.

"Yes," she said, kissing the scar above his left eye.

"Yes," she said again, moving to his cheek which had been so terribly bruised.

"Yes," she said again, finally reaching his

mouth. "Everything you say."

ALSO BY JULIET MICHAELS

A FRAGILE HEART

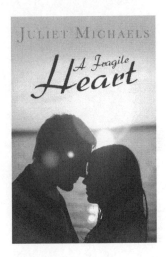

Is Elena ready to love again?

Elena Walsh is happy with her simple, quiet life. Well, most of the time. At work she keeps herself busy, and at home she has more than enough to worry about, taking care of her troublesome younger brother, Josh.

But one morning, an accident leads Elena stumbling straight into the path of Guy Silver, an intriguing, complicated man. And as Elena begins to get to know him, it becomes clear that there's more to Guy than first meets the eye, not to mention the fact that he's a billionaire ...

So why in the world does he seem interested in her? You see, Elena can't believe that someone like Guy could like her. She's always had issues with her figure, and lacks confidence in herself and others ...

Out now!

ALSO BY JULIET MICHAELS

A VENETIAN SUMMER

Who will Daisy choose?

Daisy Potts is young, carefree and single – spending her summer teaching English in the beautiful city of Venice. But her time in Italy quickly begins to heat up when she meets Salvatore, a handsome, enigmatic older man from a wealthy Venetian family.

And as the two grow close, Daisy begins to find out more about Salvatore's past, eventually leading her to a surprising discovery.

Soon Daisy's carefree summer is turned upside

down, as she is forced to confront a past relationship of her own: with Italian student Alex. Now Daisy finds herself at a crossroads: which man will she choose?

Out now!

AN IRISH PASSION

13830627R00122

Printed in Great Britain
by Amazon.co.uk, Ltd.,
Marston Gate.